ROE VALENTINE

EVERNIGHT PUBLISHING ®

www.evernightpublishing.com

Editor: Stephanie Balistreri

Cover Artist: Jay Aheer

ISBN: 978-1-77339-133-5

ROE VALENTINE

ACKNOWLEDGEMENTS

Thank you Grace Coronado and Whitney Watson for reading early versions of Playboy Assistant. Your time and thoughts mean so much to me. Many thanks to my amazing friend Teri Wilson who supports me and gives me the encouragement I need to keep going. And to my editor Stephanie for helping me refine Playboy Assistant. You women are gold! I am so grateful to you all.

ROE VALENTINE

PLAYBOY ASSISTANT

Society Playboys, 1

Roe Valentine

Copyright © 2016

Chapter One

What the hell am I doing here? In his aggravation, Fabian vowed to kill his dad if he didn't get this damned job. He gazed down at his freshly manicured fingers to reel in his rising anger. He'd rather be on his yacht, not waiting for an interview set up by his father. Talk about emasculating. His father had the brilliant idea Fabian should work elsewhere before joining the family's bioengineering firm. Apparently, he didn't care for Fabian bumming around anymore.

Two weeks prior, his dad kicked him out of the family house, which honestly was fine with him. He was tired of being served breakfast by a different stripper every morning anyhow. His dad loved his strippers. Fabian peered down at his fingers again, the hot spread of dread waving through him.

Glancing up to the metal clock on the wall, he noted the infamous Mrs. Helene Robuchon was late. Fabian took in a deep breath, cleansing the stress that continued to build inside him. The girl next to him smiled, lips stretched to a wide crescent. *Cute.* He lifted up the edge of his mouth, and silently chuckled at her blushing face. Bare crossed legs caught his attention.

Very cute. He could be too obvious with his objectifications. He might even be an asshole, but girls liked players. At least that was the impression he got by the multitude of women vying for his attention. Not that he meant to be an asshole player, it just happened. And he'd guess the only reason he got away with anything was because women generally thought he was good-looking. Apparently, Swedish and Greek genes created something women couldn't resist. And of course being born into a wealthy family didn't hurt.

"Hey," he said, putting on that Pallis charm, which meant lower tone of voice, curled lip, side-eye stare. His friends would rag on him hard for pulling that shit. The girl blushed as she squeaked a "hi". He decided she was right out of college. "You here to interview for the assistant position?"

"No. I'm an intern in the marketing department. I'm supposed to start today."

Very nice. He leaned back in the metal and leather chair, surveying her for potential. She might be too innocent for him, he surmised, studying her makeup-free face. He liked women who knew the drill. Knew how to get over it when things went south because with him they always did. His gaze dropped to her fingers clasped tight in her lap. Nude fingernails. He decided she wasn't his type after all.

"What position are you interviewing for?" she asked, once he'd turned his attention away.

Without looking at her, he said, "Executive assistant to the CEO."

"Mrs. Robuchon's assistant?" She'd lowered her voice to a whisper.

Glancing up to meet her stare, he nodded. "That's the one. And she's almost fifteen minutes late." Another glance at the clock reignited his irritation.

"I interviewed with her last month. She's a real…" She bit her bottom lip and continued, "A real tough one. I heard she's already gone through three assistants this year."

I'm going to kill my dad. "Really?" His father and Helene had been friends for over thirty years. "That's just awesome." Another five minutes passed without conversation. Just as he thought to say screw it and walk out of Robuchon Investments, a voice sounded from an open door by the reception desk.

"Mr. Pallis, please come with me."

He laughed. What timing. Only twenty-five minutes late. He left the lobby, the tap of his expensive shoes echoed off the high-gloss tiles and massive glass doors leading to the office suite. Behind the glass walls was different from the reception area. Fabian adjusted the lapels of his designer suit as he walked side-by-side with the forty-something woman, making eye contact with each employee living the cube life. The same poor excuse for an existence would surely become his reality too if he actually got this job. Not the life he thought he'd have when he was a Harvard MBA student. On a good note, most of the women he passed were decent-looking. Some were above average. More to look forward to.

At the end of the labyrinth of hallways emerged a frosted glass door taller and wider than all the other doors. Next to it was a metal plate spelling "T. Robuchon".

The woman turned to him, a smile on her face. He gazed at her lips. "Miss Robuchon will see you now." She pushed open the door.

Miss Robuchon?

He nodded, the question hanging in his head as he walked across the threshold. The office was sterile, to say the least. Glass and metal. And cold. Even in the Houston summer, he felt a chill in that office. His gaze shifted to the left, and there he took in the entirety of *Miss* Robuchon who clearly was *not* Helene, his father's friend of more than thirty years.

"You're not Helene Robuchon." He nearly choked on his surprise to see her very grown-up daughter, Antonia. Could this woman be the same girl he went to school with so long ago? He barely remembered her.

She stood before him, straight as a pin. The small, demure woman wore a conservative white pencil skirt and matching button down blouse, probably silk by the way it rippled and shimmered under the lighting. Fabian was so taken aback, he couldn't decide if she was the kind that knew the drill or not. She looked like someone who created the drill. It made him enthusiastic about the interview. She turned her face for a moment, her chocolate brown hair kissed with caramel streaks whipped over her shoulder. When she turned back to him, her full red lips were pressed into a line. And he probably looked like a damned idiot staring at her. *Get it together, Pallis.*

Sparkling dark eyes captured him. They were powerful. Standing there, tiny as she was, authority spilled from her pores. He needed a minute to contain himself, and that *never* happened.

Her smooth, cultured voice fell from her lips like music. "You may call me Miss Robuchon."

She moved gracefully to her desk, which was far too big for her. As she sat, her blouse parted a bit to show a tan collarbone. *Dear God.* A ripple of lust shot through his body. *Shit.* She'd barely said a couple of words to him and he was ready to pop off.

"I apologize, I was expecting … something else," he stuttered, trying to look smooth as he lunged to the chair across from her desk. Only a rookie would risk pitching a tent in that moment. A rookie he was not. His most pressing task was to stop looking at her chest.

She watched him intensely for a response when he caught her gaze again.

In a second flat, her gaze dropped to his lap. Her cheeks flushed immediately.

"What were you expecting?"

Shit, she saw. "I meant I was expecting someone else."

"Ah," she said, leaning back in the colossal leather chair. "My mother."

Since when did Helene have a daughter who looked like that? "Yes, your mother."

He needed to get it together. Attractive women surrounded him all the time. What the hell was his problem? Fabian had to remind himself how good he was with women. Very good. In fact, he was an expert. He knew how to talk to women. He knew how to make them swoon. But, holy shit, he was on the verge of swooning himself. Which was disconcerting.

And infuriating.

"Our parents are good friends. I should ream out my father for not setting up a playdate for us, I'd remember you a lot better if he had." Enter that Pallis charm. By the look on her face, she wasn't impressed.

A delicate hand danced over the desktop, pulling a piece of paper closer to her. She read from it, not acknowledging him, which probably was for the best. "Harvard grad, I see. The MBA program." She didn't look up for a reaction. "Also a Harvard undergrad with a bachelor's in bioengineering. That's impressive. We invest in bio-tech and medical device companies."

"Yes." It's all he could articulate. More and more, he wanted the job. It was probably a good idea to say as little as possible.

11

Finally, she lifted her gaze to his. "Yes, your father and my mother are very good friends. And if you remember, I went to boarding school in Atlanta after elementary."

"Oh, right. I remember that now. The out-of-state boarding school thing, not that our parents are friends." He groaned.

"I know my mom was looking forward to interviewing you, the 'Pallis kid'. Her words." She smirked.

Fabian didn't care for that comment. "I assure you I'm no kid." He was gaining more control.

"Clearly." She turned her attention to the paper in front of her once again. "And don't worry, you don't have to remember me, but I am very aware of who you are."

His ears tingled. "Oh, really? Do tell me who I am."

"What you do in your personal life doesn't concern me." She pinned him with her stare. Judgmental and all. She'd held a pen tight in her fist.

He didn't like where the conversation was going. Houston society wanted the bad boy story. Being a trust fund playboy was more exciting to talk about. Time to make the sale. "I guarantee I can do this job better than any other candidate you have lined up. As you can see, I did intern for a semester in London during my business program and I was also an engineering intern for two summers during my undergrad. You might as well tell me where my cube is."

Her eyebrow quirked up, a smirk on her face. "You're that confident?"

"I am that confident." His control was restored, as was the flaccid state of his erection that nearly ruined the interview.

Surprisingly, she remained calm, just unreadable enough to drive him crazy. Her eyes never left his. She was toying with him and that didn't suit. "The person I hire will take my orders without question or comment."

"I'm sure that won't be a problem as long as I don't have questions or comments in regards to your orders."

She steepled her fingers under her chin, elbows against the desk. "Luckily I am unlike my mother."

"How so?" Their stare intensified.

Dropping her hands to the desk, she said, "If I were my mother, that would have been the end of the interview."

He straightened, managing the conflicting emotions making his body hot. She was damn cocky and damn gorgeous. He wanted to hate her, but instead found himself growing more attracted to her as their apparent standoff continued. He watched her mouth, still parted from speaking. "It's good thing you're not your mother then."

She looked away. Pallis-1, Robuchon-0.

Several seconds later, she continued. "I will be acting CEO for the time being and, like my mother, I am very serious about the health of Robuchon Investments. I won't tolerate an assistant who doesn't believe in our mission or adheres to our policies."

"That seems fair." He sensed there was much more to the "acting CEO" situation than she was letting on.

"As my assistant, I will need you to be at my every beck and call. I will need you to keep tasks straight. Keep everything straight, in fact." She stood, and his eyes moved with her tiny curved hips as she walked over to the glass wall overlooking downtown Houston. She continued, still peering out the window. "It sounds very broad, but flexibility is key." Just then she turned to face him, their gazes met again. "I need you to be flexible."

Flexible. That was all she needed to say and he was shifting in his seat again, conjuring up all the ways he wanted *her* to be flexible. Doggie and reverse cowgirl were the top positions that came to mind. "I guarantee I can be flexible. But I'll need you to be flexible too, as my employer."

Lightly, she cleared her throat. "Thank you, Mr. Pallis, for coming in."

I just fucked that up. He stood tall with the acceptance he'd bombed the interview. "No, thank *you*, Miss Robuchon."

* * * *

Deep breaths. Toni didn't bother to get up and walk the arrogant Fabian Pallis to the door. If she had, he might notice her weak knees, which she wasn't inclined to show the likes of him. He was much better looking in person than she thought he'd be—or hoped. Plus, he carried this larger-than-life masculine energy that both attracted and annoyed her. Perhaps that was his best behavior. If so, she was in for some turbulence. She could easily see how he'd make a woman crazy. He'd made plenty of women insane, from what she'd heard. A friend of a friend had been dumped by him the summer before and *still* hadn't gotten over him. What kind of magical moves did he have to inspire such longing?

Toni looked at her new business cards on a tiny tripod next to her computer. *Antonia Robuchon, Acting CEO.* The title was laughable. At least it was to the eight executives who tolerated her presence. She was only twenty-five years old and not at all prepared for what had landed on her lap. To think of why she suddenly found herself acting CEO made her sad. Sad enough to let a tear fall down her cheek.

Toni picked at the small solitaire diamond necklace she wore as a thought came to her. The very thought that haunted her since she'd become acting CEO almost a month ago. Her mother would certainly die. Most died of pancreatic cancer. Toni wondered how much more her life would change when that happened. Already she'd forged a wall around herself, making her tough. Sometimes she didn't recognize herself with the hard exterior. Many times she wondered when someone would call her out.

The intercom buzzed, startling her from the deep thoughts. Disoriented, Toni blinked to get her bearings. "Yes?"

"Miss Robuchon, Mr. Pallis has been input into the system."

Toni nodded to herself. That was the plan. She had no choice in the matter. Fabian Pallis would get the job whether he deserved it or not. And the kicker was she couldn't fire him easily. He'd have to fornicate on the reception desk with an employee during business hours for him to get fired. Bottom line—she was stuck with him. For a while at least. A month? A year? She wasn't sure.

"Please inform him in the morning him he's been hired."

* * * *

In yoga class that night Toni was less stable than usual. She couldn't find balance to save her life, but sweated profusely if that was any kind of a triumph. Her mantra went something like this: *I am a Robuchon. I am tough as nails, and I will overcome all obstacles.* Letting her family down wasn't an option. When yoga class ended, she stood outside the studio waiting for Miles, her driver. The Mercedes limo wasn't where it normally was. *Marvelous.*

Her cell phone buzzed in her bag. A message from Miles popped up.

Miles: **Getting fuel. Will be there shortly. Please accept my apologies.**

She pursed her lips.

Me: **That should be done on your time, Miles. Please hurry.**

Sounded like something her mom would say. Fitting, though. After all, she had essentially stepped in her place.

"T. Robuchon."

The familiar voice sounded from behind her. She turned, hoping the voice did not belong to Fabian Pallis. Unfortunately, it did. *Double marvelous.* He stood, towering over her, dressed in cycling gear.

She groaned, both embarrassed and annoyed with seeing him. "What the hell are you doing here?" Taking him in, she couldn't deny he looked utterly gorgeous standing there like that. Her assistant was hot. He had no idea she was his boss, and she wasn't going to tell him then either. She frowned. Just because it was afterhours didn't mean she would soften toward him—or any of the employees. They must always be professional.

He laughed, adjusting his stance. Toni glanced down to his crotch, lifting her gaze just as quick. But he'd caught her checking him out. *For God's sake.* Her face grew hot while his stupid smile grew wider. The jerk. Sparkling green eyes accompanied that smile, which unfortunately made her insides swish about, activating feelings that had been dormant for the better part of a year. Why couldn't she stop looking at his crotch?

He laughed again, filling the awkward silence that stretched between her question and his answer. "I live on the sixth floor." He pointed above the yoga studio. The complex was the newest retail/residential space in

Midtown backed by the real estate leg of Pallis Enterprises. He openly checked her out in her own spandex outfit, eyes lingering on her bosom. "Yoga girl, I see."

She straightened her spine, tightening her throat column. He needed to know he couldn't be so familiar with her. "Mr. Pallis, I'm a woman, not a girl. And yes, I do enjoy yoga."

He chuckled, the smile meeting his eyes. "Clearly. Very much a woman." He winked. The memory of their earlier conversation came to her mind.

Toni's cheeks heated further with the inflection in his tone and the way his eyes narrowed with the insinuation.

"So what's the 'T' stand for?" She watched the curve of his lips as he spoke, and mirrored his tilted head.

"Toni."

"Toni…" he said, elongating the last syllable. He smiled at her, and she liked it.

Damn, he's good. She straightened. Nope, he wouldn't gain any power over her. "I'm known as Miss Robuchon at RI."

"We don't have to be so formal. I mean, I don't work for you, do I?" He winked.

Toni put a fist to her hip. "How dare you sweet talk me into divulging if you got the job or not."

He raised an eyebrow in that cocky way she didn't like—all sure of himself. "I don't have to sweet talk a girl to do anything, Toni."

"Don't call me that." She was annoyed. Beyond annoyed, and knew full well her reaction was disproportionate to what happened, which was nothing really.

"I tell you what…" He smiled down at her, and she could have sworn he stepped close enough for her to smell the sweat off his skin. "If you become my boss, I'll call you Miss Robuchon. Deal?" Yes, he definitely was closer. He lowered his face to hers, and then she could smell his breath, which wasn't bad. It was sweet. And warm. Much like her body, ready to combust being so close to him.

"I—" Just as she was recklessly going to agree, Miles drove up. She lunged toward the limo. "I have to go."

Dear God, what is wrong with me? She leaped toward the door, jumping in like some escaped convict and slammed it shut. Once in the backseat, she gasped for air, grateful for the presidential tint windows. Fabian didn't need to see what a mess she was. He stared in the window though, trying to look inside. His parted lips made her knees weak again, doing terrible things to her imagination, which prompted her gaze to fall to his crotch again.

"Hurry, Miles. I need to get home right now."

Mile's dark eyes reflected back from the rearview mirror. "Yes, ma'am. I'm sorry about the wait."

"Please be on time from now on," she said, containing herself. But not really. Groaning, she slid down the backseat until the edge of the tan leather seat fit in the middle of her back and her knees hit the floorboard.

In her Museum District penthouse, she stood in front of the mirror in her master bathroom. Mary had cleaned the mirror to a sparkling perfection only to be fogged by the steam coming from the running shower. She stripped off her yoga clothes, sighing at her reflection, Fabian Pallis still on her mind. Those green eyes. Those broad shoulders and hands made to hold a woman. She bit her bottom lip and thought of all the things he could probably do to her in the bedroom. And all the ways she would like it. It had been a long time. Obviously.

Men and what they could do in the bedroom had been the furthest thing from her mind. Especially after Stephan. She needed to focus on her mother and the fact that she was acting CEO. Life had thrown her a curveball. This wasn't what she expected. If life had gone by the playbook, she would be Stephan's wife. Probably thinking about being a mother, too. What she wouldn't be was a CEO—acting CEO. Truth was, Toni hadn't been groomed to work in any capacity. All her grooming was to prepare her to be a trophy wife. That was a fact, whether she liked it or not. Not knowing otherwise, she was happy to fill the role of wife. Until she was forced into the workforce. Until she saw what freedom it was to work and to contribute in some real way. Every day for nearly a month she'd walked into Robuchon Investments as a businesswoman with free will. She'd actually started to believe she might have a knack for it. Trouble was, how would she convince anyone else?

Her gaze fell to her bare feet, still smooth from her weekly pedicure. "Mary," she called and moments later her housekeeper appeared at the door, ignoring the fact she was still naked. It didn't matter though. Mary had taken care of Toni since she was a baby. Right out of the hospital room.

"How may I assist, Miss Robuchon?" A woman of near fifty-five years old, she stood straight as a pin with her arms at her side. Out of habit, she wore black slacks and a white button-down shirt, with hair pulled back into a chignon. Toni's mother preferred that uniform.

"Can you please warm my towels? I'm feeling a bit of a chill." Toni smiled as she nodded.

"Of course, ma'am. Anything else?"

She turned from the opened glass shower door. "I'll take a cup of chamomile tea with honey and lemon after my shower."

"Very well." Mary nodded again, turning and disappearing into her master suite.

Toni stepped into the steam-filled shower, breathing in until her lungs ached. As much as she wanted him out of her mind, she imagined Fabian standing with her under the waterfall showerhead, piercing her with not just his eyes. A serious question hung in the air… How would she survive this CEO thing with a playboy assistant?

Chapter Two

God, I've got to change that damn ring. Fabian had been deep in the throes of a dirty dream—filthy actually—featuring Toni Robuchon and he didn't want it to end. On the screen of the screaming phone, he read, *Robuchon Investments.* Shooting up from the bed, he answered the call.

"Hello?" he said it in his best I-wasn't-asleep voice possible.

"May I speak to Mr. Pallis?" Her voice was smooth. She'd obviously been awake for hours.

"Yes … speaking." His heart pounded wildly. All the images of Toni in some of his favorite positions fled, including the accompanying morning wood.

"This is the hiring manager for Robuchon Investments." She paused.

"I hope you have good news for me."

"Yes, I believe I do. We would like to offer you the position of executive assistant to Miss Antonia Robuchon."

Seriously? Didn't he royally screw up that interview? At least that was the impression he got last night when ran into the CEO herself. Or acting CEO, that is. "No shit? I mean, really?"

"Yes, sir," she continued in her professional manner.

"Do I get paid time off?" What a stupid question. He groaned. His dad would be so proud.

She hesitated. He could hear shuffling paper in the background. "Yes, you do. When can you come in to further discuss the details and fill out your paperwork? That is, if you intend on accepting the offer…"

"I definitely intend on accepting the offer."

Fabian smiled, picturing Toni in her yoga outfit and naked in his dream. He glanced at the clock across his dark bedroom. Nearly ten in the morning. No more sleeping in. No more cruising out on the Gulf in his yacht. No more all the things he liked to do with his mornings since he came back from Cambridge. "I can go in this afternoon. About two or so?"

"I'll schedule you for two-thirty."

Fabian rubbed his matted hair. "I'll be there." *And I get to see the sexy boss lady in real time.* He'd found a replacement for all the things he liked to do with his mornings.

"Thank you, Mr. Pallis. We'll see you soon." She hung up before he could respond.

Still holding the phone to his ear, Fabian laughed. "Holy shit." He still couldn't believe it. Somehow he knew his life was about to change drastically. Without thinking twice, he selected his dad's number from the list of contacts in his cell phone. His anxiety grew exponentially with each ring. He hated speaking to him. Even if to tell him good news.

"Vicky's phone," the high-pitched voice answered. Another of his dad's hookers. Or strippers. If she was older than eighteen, Fabian would be surprised.

"Where's my dad?" Fabian didn't hide his annoyance. Too many women came in and out of his father's life—his too. He'd always wondered if that was the reason his mom left him—and Fabian—all those years ago.

She squealed. Fabian removed the phone from his ear for a moment. "Is this Fabie?"

"It's Fabian, not Fabie. And tone it down on the squealing." She squealed again. That time louder, making him cringe like she'd ran her fingernails down a very long chalkboard. What the hell was going on over there?

Good thing he'd left his father's house permanently. That whole scene made him sick to his stomach. He'd never live in the same house with him again. "Just get my dad on the phone."

"Aw! Someone sounds like a grumpy-pants." She laughed.

The blood heated his body, coursing through him like a strong current. "Anyone tell you it's rude to answer someone else's phone?"

"Fabian, what is it? I'm busy." Annoyed as usual when he spoke to Fabian, his father's voice filled the space in the abrupt way he did everything.

"So is that the same adult entertainer as yesterday? I know you like to swap them out." Triumph for Fabian. He knew how much his father hated his commentary about all the women his father bedded.

"Watch your mouth." His dad might have been a bit drunk by the subtle slur. Typical. "The only thing you should be calling me for is to tell me you got the job at RI. Your trust fund won't last forever with the way you're burning through it."

At every turn, Fabian's father threw his trust fund in his face. What was it for if not to spend? And besides, his father had no room to judge. He had his own trust fund as well. "Thanks for reminding me. Again. And I *did* get the job at RI working for Antonia."

"Antonia? Helene's daughter?" His father sobered with the question. "Why are you working for Antonia?"

Fabian threw the sheets off his legs, standing from the bed. "Apparently Antonia is the acting CEO."

"Antonia is a damn kid, like you."

His free hand balled into a fist. "Well, she's CEO. Acting CEO, whatever the hell that means." He would always just be a damn kid to his father.

"This is going to be a disaster. What the hell was

Helene thinking?" His father paused a moment. "That wasn't the agreement."

His ears perked up. "What do you mean, *agreement*?" He should have known there was more to this job than his father was letting on.

His father grunted, completely ignoring the question. "You have a lot to prove to me, Fabian. You've been gallivanting around on your yacht since you left Harvard. You think everything is just going to be handed to you."

"You're getting awfully self-righteous, Dad. Everything *was* handed to you." His face was like a furnace, hot to the point of explosion. Confrontations with his father always ruined his day. Every time.

"I worked and invested. I never went out blowing my trust fund on luxuries when I was your age."

"You just waited until Mom left you. Or maybe that's why she left you." Too much. The icy silence followed confirmed Fabian had gone too far.

"You have anything else to say?"

Fabian turned on his heels, gripping the tiles with his toes as he walked the length of the king-sized bed. He wanted to say he was sorry, but he just couldn't. "Nothing else."

His father hung up without saying goodbye. Business as usual.

The potent ache of defeat worked through his body. It hadn't in a long time, at least not like that. He'd done everything his dad wanted, studied at his alma mater, obtained engineering and business degrees, had been awarded magna cum laude, surprising to most people, and still it wasn't enough. He tossed the phone on the side table, walking toward the wall panel where the drape switch was nestled between the light and ceiling fan switches. Slowly, the room filled with light as the drapes slid open along the full length of the wall. He squinted until he could take the full force of the sun.

I can do this job. He had no other choice than to prove to his dad he was responsible and not some useless twenty-six-year-old trust fund brat.

* * * *

Fabian glanced at his IWC watch. The long hand was just about to strike the six as he approached the glass reception desk at Robuchon Investments. The receptionist looked up from the switchboard. He flashed his Pallis smile, eliciting a blush to her cheeks. "I'm Fabian Pallis. HR is expecting me."

Her full mouth pulled in a seductive smile. *Good lips.* "Yes, I know who you are, Mr. Pallis." She stood, giving him a full view of her even more attractive body. Round breasts and cinched waist. When his gaze lifted from her cleavage to meet her eyes, he was greeted with an even larger smile—if that were possible. "I'll be more than happy to escort you to HR."

"That'll be all, Davina. I'll escort Mr. Pallis, thank you." The melodic voice startled him.

He turned to Toni, her narrowed eyes judging him. Clearly, she was immune to the Pallis smile.

Davina spoke before he could. "Toni, you scared me."

"Miss Robuchon, Davina."

"Of course, Miss Robuchon, I apologize." Davina sat again. Anything else she did after was completely unimportant to Fabian. He'd set his eyes on the woman before him.

What a hard-ass. A jolt of excitement rushed through him. His gaze fell down her svelte body. Everything about her shape pleased him. Her fire engine red dress. Her perfectly curved hips. Her narrow waist. He imagined he could wrap one hand around that tiny waist. But, he did have a rather large hand. He had other large things too. One specific thing would get larger if he kept imagining picking her up by her waist, like he'd done in the very explicit dream he'd had of her. His gaze lifted to her face, admiring her pulled back hair that accentuated her dainty bone structure. And her lips… Her lips stood out like red pillows ready to suck him in. He could be sucked in by her. Easily.

God, she's gorgeous. More than gorgeous. She was a goddess.

"Come with me, Mr. Pallis." Her dark eyes gripped him for a moment before she turned toward the open glass door. Fabian glanced to Davina, forgetting she'd been there. In the span of a minute, she lost her appeal. He imagined all women would lose their appeal standing next to Antonia Robuchon.

* * * *

Fabian's Tom Ford cologne—her favorite men's cologne—danced in Toni's nose as he passed inside her office. Even in her four-inch heels, he was still at least ten inches taller than her. Not to mention large like an athlete with thick soccer player thighs. A fleeting memory came of him playing soccer in PE class in the fourth grade. They'd been just kids then. Now, he was all grown up. He brushed her arm as he passed, shooting electricity through her body and straight to her nether regions she wished would stop reacting to him.

After he passed, she released the door, making her way to the other side of the desk. His eyes were on her as she walked by him, and his energy kneaded her body with each step. His sex appeal was much more potent than she expected. She could not have prepared herself for the power that radiated off him. Mother Nature had clearly played favorites with him. Damned Mother Nature.

"So 'T. Robuchon', huh?" There was amusement in his voice she didn't care for.

Toni busied herself with shuffling papers, and ignoring his question. She hadn't gone by Toni until middle school. Again, she looked at him—below the belt. It was hard to not notice the way his thigh muscles pulled at his trousers as he sat. Mother Nature created a monster. He was entirely too good-looking in that suit—too good-looking in general.

"It's really irrelevant to you. You will address me as Miss Robuchon, remember?"

His chuckle irked her. "Okay, *Miss* Robuchon. We did have a deal, after all." He leaned back in the chair, reminding her of their conversation in front of the yoga studio. And it was a struggle not to look at his crotch. "Well, then, since we're on such formal terms, I think it's appropriate that you address me as Mr. Pallis. Or 'sir'." A lick of his lips stirred her desire. They were starting off on the wrong foot. And it was only day one.

As calm as her mother would have been, she crossed her arms over her chest, meeting his intense gaze until it became a competition. She refused to look away, and clearly he did too.

"You grew up to be cocky, didn't you? Though I shouldn't be surprised. You're a bit of a celebrity in certain circles." He was getting to her.

He leaned back. "Your circle?"

"Hardly." She dismissed him, looking away again to her business cards still sitting on that tiny tripod. She hadn't given a single card to anyone yet. When she looked back at him, he was smirking. She, on the other hand, was ready to get to business. His personal life wasn't her affair anyhow. "Robuchon Investments is delighted you've accepted the offer to be my assistant."

"We both know this is a fake job, right?"

Yes, it was a fake job. But she couldn't tell him that. They'd obviously been put in unconventional positions. "I wouldn't say anything about your employment is fake, Mr. Pallis. As long as you are serious about working."

He was brooding then. "As long as you report favorably to my father."

She stood and walked toward the refreshment cart near the door, shaking the whole way there. "I don't know what you mean. You'll be treated like a typical employee. No better. No worse." She poured herself a glass of iced tea, and barely managed to get the packet of raw cane sugar open with her trembling fingers.

"I doubt that," he said, his voice sounding close behind her.

Toni held her breath, not daring to turn. The heat of his body grabbed her. She took a sip only to keep her hands—and mouth—busy. Hotter still, he invaded her space until she finally turned. Only inches from her, his jaw clenched. For a moment, she thought he might bend down to kiss her. He didn't, but her heart raced as if he had.

"So what's the deal with my father?"

Toni took another sip, forcing the cold liquid down her steaming insides. She really could faint if he didn't back away. One of them really should back away. "I don't know what you mean." But there was a deal. Hire Fabian Pallis. And she did, despite the fact that he was not assistant material.

His eyebrows furrowed, and she saw every hair on his face. Did he get closer? "So I got this job fair and square?"

"Yes." She was barely able to get the single word out. For God's sake, it was just one syllable. Somehow she managed to set her cup down without it slipping through her fingers and breaking on the tiles. He didn't believe her weak "yes". Neither did she. But they were standing there, so close, and he probed her with his eyes in every way a person could be without actually touching. She gulped, and said again, "Yes. You did."

Fabian laughed at the absurdity of it. Minty breath smothered her face. Obviously, he knew he didn't get the job fair and square. He leaned in a bit more. Yes, it was possible. She braced herself. *He's going to kiss me*. He didn't kiss her, though. To make matters more absurd, she wanted him to kiss her. Instead, he said, "Then tell me how I'm qualified."

"Uh…" *Need to get away from him*. Somehow, she unwedged herself from between him and the beverage cart. She gathered more strength the farther away she distanced herself from him. "You're starting off on the wrong foot, Mr. Pallis."

"Look, I know my father and your mom have some sort of arrangement for me to work here until I can prove to the old man I'm not the idiot he thinks I am."

Toni crossed her arms. "Probably just a good idea to play along if you want to leave here anytime soon."

His chuckle surprised her. "Is there another choice?"

She looked in his eyes. "No, I don't think there is."

After Fabian left her office to fill out paperwork, she dialed her mother's landline. The interaction was still fresh in her mind, especially the part where he could have kissed her. She was throbbing all over with the memory and it wasn't going to subside anytime soon. Just as she began to wonder what *if* he had kissed her, her mother's nurse answered the phone.

"Ms. Keller, it's Toni. Is my mother available?" Toni stared at the door for several moments while she waited on the line. She imagined Fabian's large body filling the doorframe. *Stop thinking about him.* He wouldn't dare come into her office without knocking, would he? She panicked, knowing he was the type that would.

Pull yourself together.

"Antonia." Her mother's voice was weak and broken from the pain she undoubtedly had been in. Chemotherapy wasn't for the weak. Her mother had always been strong.

"Hi, Mom. How are you?"

"They say I'm dying."

Toni's chest ached like someone punched her. "Don't say that."

"The question is, how are you? Have you completely destroyed RI yet?"

Toni laughed only because she knew her mother really meant it. "It's not even been month yet, Mom. RI is still standing."

"Did you hire the Pallis kid like I told you to?"

"I did. But, I'm just not sure it's a good idea. I don't think he … respects my authority." How else could she describe it? Not that she had any intentions of telling her mother what happened near the beverage cart. Nope. Neither parents would ever know about that.

"He's your age and a man. Men don't like reporting to women. It's a fact. But I had to take over RI when your father died. Remember?"

She nodded, a lump lodged in her throat. "Mm-hm."

"You'll be fine. Just have him do busy work. Organize your social calendar. Things like that. The execs will keep the business together. And if you really get in a bind, you know to call me. I owe Victor this favor. It won't be for long."

"Exactly how long? I just don't know how long I can take it." She bit her bottom lip, imaging Fabian sitting in her guest chair, practically busting out of it with his size. His size… *Oh God.* First thing's first, she needed to stop imagining him—or his size—in any capacity if this arrangement had any chance of going over without a hitch. Besides, she despised womanizers.

"You just hired the kid. What the hell could have possibly gone wrong already?" Her mother coughed several times, making Toni's trouble with the young Pallis seem so trivial.

"Please, Mom, get some rest. Don't worry about it. I'll be okay."

"Yes, I think I will get some rest. This chemo isn't quite what I thought. I don't think anyone could have prepared me for this ordeal."

"Mom, please take it easy."

She coughed again. "Sometimes life gives you the thing you never thought you'd need. And takes away the thing you thought you'd always have."

Toni thought of Stephan Bradley. Heir to the Bradley fortune. Her ex-fiancé who dumped her for another woman almost a year to the date. Her gaze shifted to the computer screen calendar. Yes, she would be getting married next weekend had it all worked out. Anger took over, as it had every time she thought of all the years she wasted on him. "You're right, Mom. Nothing is ever guaranteed."

Chapter Three

Goddess in a red dress. That was all Fabian could think about, even with Camille walking around his apartment in her white lacey thong. Her tan skin contrasted the scant white material in the best way. But it didn't matter. All he could think about was how Toni would look in that thong. Fabian reclined on his oversized couch, watching Camille as she slipped off her bra, her breasts springing out to tempt him.

"Not in the mood, Cam," he said, tilting his head to see past her as she paraded in front of him. She attempted to straddle him—that was her move. And he normally liked it.

Camille pouted, hands resting on top of her hip bones. "Why?" He hated when she whined.

She pressed her chest against his face. With both hands, he took a hold of her hips and moved her to the side. "Not now, Camille."

"Fine." She crossed her arms over her bare chest, a frown formed on her usually pretty face. "You've been acting weird all day. What's going on with you?"

He focused on the television, and though he didn't know what he was watching he feigned interest. His skin prickled the longer Camille stood before him. "I have to be in the office early tomorrow. You should leave now."

She grew frantic. "What do you mean?" He'd never asked her to leave before. Actually, they would have been on their second round of sex had he not been forced to work for Robuchon Investments. More specifically, for Antonia Robuchon.

"Camille, you're not my girlfriend. You know I'm not looking for anything serious." He didn't look at her and was met with her silence. That was the part he hated the most, reminding women he wasn't on the relationship market when they started to get too close.

"So the last four months meant nothing to you?" As fast as they were off, her clothes appeared back on her body.

He sighed, dipping his head a moment before he met her angry blue stare. "Camille, it hasn't meant nothing. We've had fun, right?"

"And that's all you wanted. Fun?"

He watched as she grabbed her purse. "I told you I didn't want a serious thing."

"Well…" She smoothed down her micro dress. "Have fun not having a serious thing!" Pivoting on her heels, she traveled across the wide living room to the front door of his sixth-floor condo. With one last look shooting arrows into him, she yanked open the door and slammed it. The vibrations traveled over the floor to his feet planted on the hardwood. He groaned.

Left with nothing but the television noise, he squeezed his eyes shut. *Shit*. He leaned back further into the couch cushions, burrowing in them. Not long after he found a comfortable spot, his pocket vibrated. Groaning, he reached in his jeans back pocket and pulled out the phone.

SweetTina: **Want some company?**

He sighed. How had he kept all these women straight? And separate? He reread the question, answering with one simple word.

Fabian: **Nope**.

Sweet Tina. She really was sweet. And she didn't care that he had other women. Tina might have had a boyfriend, but Fabian wasn't sure and didn't care. Actually, that worked best for him. It had, anyway. For some reason, he imagined Toni sitting in that large executive chair staring at him with judgment in her eyes.

He'd actually started to feel shame about all the women he had on rotation.

SweetTina: **Too bad. You know where I am if you change your mind, handsome.**

He didn't respond. Instead, he tossed the phone across the room, partially wanting it to break, but was glad when it landed on the square ottoman pressed against the opposite wall. Damn his dad for making him work for Antonia Robuchon. She wasn't someone he could casually call for some Netflix and chill. His cocky side wanted to try, but another part of him knew that wouldn't go over well.

"You're being stupid, Pallis." Why the hell would he want her? She was his boss and probably didn't like him much anyway. It was completely ridiculous. Still … he wanted her to like him. In some way. In a way that let him know she didn't think he was a complete jerk.

Standing, he tossed the throw pillow back on the couch. He just needed some rest. Tomorrow he'd start his assistant gig officially, and he wanted to be fresh. He wanted to prove he could be responsible and not the womanizing indulgent prick his father—and maybe everyone else—thought he was. He frowned at the thought, Toni's judgmental stare still in his mind.

* * * *

Toni sat at the massive desk where her mother had sat for ten years, and her father had sat for many years before that. She never thought she'd find herself sitting in that desk. It was almost midnight and she still hadn't left Robuchon Investments. She'd been compiling data on a startup medical company seeking capital for a clinical study. The executives had tossed out the proposal, deeming it too risky. But after Toni had researched the technology, she thought it was worth another look. Though the executives had reminded her of her very temporary place at RI, she started to dismiss their dismissal and believe she had something to offer, which she'd never thought she would in a professional capacity. And more than that, she actually wanted to offer something. Now that she was single with no husband in sight, she needed to get on her own feet, though she knew her mother wouldn't take too kindly to her decision. If she could ever muster the nerve to tell her.

After she'd written the last paragraph of her proposal, she put the folder aside and stared at her computer. Images of her father circled the screen. Her mother kept those old pictures from before his untimely death, a heart attack that shocked everyone. Up next on the screen was her father in a canoe on Lake Travis. Next, he was in the backyard of their River Oaks mansion manning the grill because he liked to do "regular people" things even though he was brought up in old money wealth most people could only dream of. Her father was the complete opposite of her mother. She was uppity. Demanding. Wanted to be treated like royalty. And she always had been.

Her gaze fell to the taskbar at the bottom of the screen. The email she'd received from Victor Pallis, Fabian's father, was minimized hours ago when she received it. With a deep sigh, she navigated the mouse arrow over the email icon and double-clicked. The email filled the entire width and height of the screen.

To: Toni Robuchon (t.robuchon@robuchoninvestments.biz)
From: Victor Pallis (Victor@PEngineering.biz)
Date: Tuesday, July 12
RE: Fabian
Antonia—I was rather surprised to hear that you hired my son, instead of Helene. I hope she is well. However, I trust the agreement I had with your mother is

still valid.

The purpose of this mock employment is two-fold. I need Fabian to straighten up in his personal life. And last, I need Fabian to prove to me that he is responsible. He must show me he is capable in business before I will make him a partner at Pallis Engineering. I'm sure you understand the importance as your mother does, hence our agreement. I ask that you not go easy on Fabian. He is used to getting his way with women, I must warn you. This must be a strictly professional relationship between you two. I'm sure you can behave in such a manner.

Every week I require a full report on his behavior. Your mother has agreed to this, and I expect you to communicate with me regularly. Should you have any questions about this arrangement, please speak to your mother. Otherwise, I expect the first report in the beginning of next week.

Sincerely,
Victor Pallis
President, Managing Partner
Pallis Engineering

She read the email again, and again. She read it until she practically memorized it. *He is used to getting his way with women, I must warn you*. She snorted. No doubt there. Especially after what happened in her office with the *near* kiss. She imagined him. His handsome-assin face. His gorgeous green eyes. His body that was the epitome of what a man should be. Over six-feet-tall and thick in every way. She closed her eyes, feeling the rush of sensation course through her body. She hated how he made her feel. All ready and wanting a man. But that only reminded her of her ex-fiancé. With that, her anger grew and she wondered exactly how much Fabian was used to getting his way with women.

Leaning toward the keyboard, she typed in "Fabian Pallis" in the search engine box. *Why am I doing this?* She should have learned her lesson when she stalked him after his interview. At first, she looked away as the results churned out in rapid speed, her heart pounding.

A quick lick to both lips and she shifted her gaze to take in the search results. First, her attention went to the many photos under the images tab. As if an otherworldly force moved her fingers, she grabbed the mouse and clicked to display the tile of images. There were hundreds of them. Some she'd already seen. Others she didn't. Pictures of him on a yacht, with bikini-clad girls, of course, popped up. On the next page of images, he was at various clubs, surrounded by a multitude of more scantily clad women. Why did she hate what she saw so much? He was no one to her. Never would be. He was a playboy. The proof was staring her in the face. Another photo caught her eye. It was him dressed in graduation robes and honor sashes from Harvard. Magna cum laude. She stared at that one longer than the others. He couldn't possibly be an idiot with that kind of honor from an Ivy League school.

Toni held her breath as she clicked on the arrow to navigate to the next page of images. Nothing but women of all types posed with him. Some looked a bit cozy, and some looked possessive. Toni's gaze fell on a picture in which he was sandwiched between two buxom blondes, and he held their waists in a way that she knew he *knew* them. She frowned. Did he *know* all those women? There were hundreds of them. *Oh, God.*

After studying a few more photos, she clicked on the web tab. The first line of the search engine read *Houston Chronicle Society, Are Fabian Pallis, 26, and Camille Carano, 23, an item?* Toni shifted her stare to the accompanying thumbnail image. The image was from a month ago. Fabian embraced a tall, gorgeous—probably a model—woman's shoulders. Her tan, splayed fingers were a bit too low on his stomach. Toni's gaze zeroed in on that part.

On the next line of the search engine, another *Houston Chronicle Society* page headline displayed *Houston playboy graduates Harvard Business School, returns home to take over family bioengineering firm.* That was a year and a half ago.

There were many more pages to read, but she just couldn't bring herself to continue. Everything she'd heard about him was true. The proof was staring her in the face. He was indeed the womanizing playboy everyone said. And this Camille Carano was a … girlfriend? One of many girlfriends? She shifted in her chair, the questions not sitting well with her. And why for the love of God could she not forget the incident in her office earlier? *Ugh.* How long would Fabian have to be her fake assistant?

Her gaze lifted to the screen again. This time, she searched for the clock on the right hand of the taskbar. *Time to go home.* Tomorrow her playboy assistant, who had a multitude of girlfriends, would start officially, and probably make her life hell, the cocky bastard. She clenched her jaw when her ex-fiancé, Stephan, infiltrated her mind again. Speaking of playboy cocky bastards… She balled her fists with the thought. Oh, she would be hard on Fabian all right. Damn how gorgeous he was. He would finally know what it was like to *not* get his way.

Chapter Four

Fabian walked into the Robuchon Investments offices like he owned the place. He walked into every place that way, but today he was feeling especially confident. Secretly, he wanted to impress Toni. His pulse raced at his throat. The Tom Ford bow tie might have been too snug, though. He'd tugged at it every few minutes since he'd left his condo. With two fingers between the shirt and tie, he yanked until he didn't feel like he was choking. In the process, he didn't see Davina approach until she was practically in his face, smiling with her artificially plumped lips pulling her shiny face. Her bosom bounced with her movements.

"Mr. Pallis, hello again," she greeted with a hand stretched out. A cascade of light brown curls fell over one shoulder.

He took her hand, noticing its warmth as they shook hands for probably too long. "Mr. Pallis is my bastard father. You can call me Fabian. I'm not formal." He laughed to make her comfortable about his backhanded comment, though his father was very much a bastard.

"Fabian." Her scent circled his nose. Cotton candy or something sweet. Something she bought at Victoria's Secret, he was certain. She flattened her palms against her wide hips, wiping them. "I was asked to show you around the office."

Fabian smiled. Not his Pallis side-smile, but still she blushed. "I've seen the office, sweetheart."

She giggled, putting a perfectly manicured hand to her lips. "More specifically, the breakroom, the supply room, and your office."

His eyebrow quirked up. "You mean I don't have

to live in a glass cube?" He scanned the equally spaced glass wall compartments filled with employees down the long space.

"Miss Robuchon wants you in the small office adjacent to hers. It was a small filing room used by Mrs. Robuchon, her mother." She frowned. "Are you not pleased?"

"Not pleased? I'm fucking ecstatic!" *Too much, Pallis.* "I mean, yeah, whatever, that's fine." She smiled, containing a laugh. She pivoted, insinuating he follow her, but he stopped. "Where is *Mrs.* Robuchon anyhow?" Odd that she hadn't been around.

Davina turned back, her expression blank. "Mrs. Robuchon has been on leave for a personal matter. Toni is stepping in temporarily. That is what we've been told, at any rate."

"Toni?" He didn't know why he asked that.

"I mean Miss Robuchon. She wants us to address her that way. But, most of us refer to her as Toni when she's not around. Some of us have known her since Mr. Robuchon would bring her into work years ago." Her eyes widened. "Don't tell her that though."

"Your secret is safe with me." He winked, prompting another blush from her pale face before she once again turned and he followed her down the hall.

Both the breakroom and the supply closet were riveting, if riveting meant boring. He had no interest in the different type of pen tips or lined notepads. Davina left him in the supply room a few minutes and returned with a cup of coffee in her grip.

"This is for Miss Robuchon. She likes exactly three-fourths cup of French roast coffee, one-fourth cup organic skim milk and three packets of raw cane sugar." She held out the cup as if everything she said wasn't completely ridiculous.

"Umm, what?" Fabian felt confused, the skin creasing between his eyes.

"She's very specific. But, she'll make you do it over until it's right." Spoken like a person who'd experienced Miss Robuchon's coffee wrath.

He took the cup, staring down into the light brown liquid. *She's got to be shitting me.* "I'm supposed to make this for her every morning?"

Davina's gaze fell to the coffee cup in his hands. "She takes it every morning at eight-fifteen. Exactly eight-fifteen."

The first problem, making coffee was not in his skill set. How would Miss Robuchon handle the deficiency? "Does she now?" He lifted the cup to his lips, and not a single hesitation went through his mind as he took a long sip. Davina gasped as the warm liquid went down his throat. "A bit cold and sweet for my taste."

"Is that right?" The silky voice came from the doorway. Toni stood, arms crossed over her tiny body dressed in a tight navy dress from shoulder to knee. Even though her feet were tucked into high nude stiletto heels, she didn't seem to fill the door space much at all. He would be surprised if she was five feet two inches without heels. "Well, it isn't for you, Mr. Pallis. It's for me. It is my taste. And you will make it for me exactly as I instruct every morning."

He stared into her dark eyes. Gorgeous or not, he had to put his foot down. "I'm not making your coffee in the morning. Do I look like a barista?"

"You're wearing a bowtie. So ... yes." Her painted red lips pressed together. For the briefest moment, he thought she might laugh. She didn't.

"Would you like me to take it off?" He challenged her with his stare.

Without looking at Davina, Antonia said, "Thank

you, Davina, you may resume your duties at reception."

"Yes, ma'am." She scurried away like a mouse, passing Antonia as she crossed to the other side.

His heart pounded as Toni strode inside the supply closet, closer to him. A wicked smile pulled her lips, but the blaze in her eyes proved she wasn't amused in the least. "This doesn't seem like a very good start to being my assistant, does it?"

He snorted. How could that small of a person change the air around him so drastically? Make him so tense? She had entirely too much power. That was going to stop. "I'll do what you want, Toni—"

"Miss Robuchon." Her lips pursed and she grew closer still.

"Miss Robuchon. Hell, I'll feed you grapes, but I'm not going to make your coffee." Their stares jousted. She'd come to a complete stop about a foot from him. All he smelled was vanilla standing so close to her.

Her jaw clenched, but she finally relented. "Fine. Don't make my coffee. Con someone else to make it. But you will deliver it to me at precisely eight-fifteen." She wasn't going to let up.

Several intense seconds passed, and then *he* relented. Annoyed with himself, he said, "Fine." Robuchon 1, Pallis 0. He let her win that round. Too easily, he might add. But there was something inside him that wanted to give her her way, which was odd since he was used to getting his. Obviously, he would have to pick his battles, though she clearly intended to fight every single one where he was concerned. She needed to show her dominance. That was fine. He could let her do that. To a point. She could think he was her whipping boy for as long as his father wanted him to be. When she wasn't his boss anymore? All bets were off when that day came.

She smirked that time, snatching the coffee cup

from his loose grip. Coffee spilled onto his suit jacket. "Oh, sorry. You can dry clean that using your expense account."

He brushed off the cold drops from his suit. "Sweetheart, I probably have more suits in my closet than you have thousand-dollar shoes."

She frowned. "It's Miss Robuchon."

"Miss Robuchon." They stared a few moments more. Was it always going to be a struggle with her? His gaze fell over her tight face. If it were possible, she might have been even more attractive. "You have something against me."

"Oh?" She seemed amused, but she wasn't fooling anyone. "Now why would you say that?"

"It's obvious. You're being a hard-ass for no reason." He was treading on thin ice and he knew it straight away. But he was running on adrenaline alone.

She crossed her arms. "Am I being a hard-ass? Or maybe you're just upset I'm not another woman to swoon in your presence?"

Her anger propelled him, which was a bad idea. "So you do have something against me. But you don't even know me."

"I know you, Mr. Pallis. Every woman in Houston knows you, apparently." Her lips snapped shut, her eyes grew larger by the second. He was getting to her. Fabian waited for her to say more, but she didn't.

"I thought you said my personal life is not your concern." He would bet his yacht she looked him up on the internet. She had to have, with that look in her eyes. But the thought made his mind reel in unprofessional ways. Why would she look him up if she wasn't interested in some way? She didn't seem the type to cyber-stalk.

Her mouth parted, and he was hanging on every

moment. His stomach rippled when her tongue licked her bottom lip. In a voice huskier than before, she said, "It's not my concern. My only concern is that you act in a professional manner when you are working for me. Now let's go to my office. I have a task for you." She turned quickly, rushing to change the subject it would seem.

"Fine by me." He wasn't done with her yet.

* * * *

This damn dress. It was too tight. Bodycon dresses were a terrible idea if a person was acting CEO. Especially when said person had an assistant who looked at the dress like he wanted to know what was under it. Because he did look at her that way. And why wouldn't he? Fabian Pallis was a player. Toni recalled all the women he'd been photographed with on the internet. It was probably a requirement to look at all women the way he looked at her in the supply room. *Focus.* Why was it so hard to focus when she could smell him again? She could feel him so close behind her again. Like when he was behind her at the beverage cart. Dear God, would she ever forget that stupid beverage cart incident?

Finally, they arrived in her office. She pushed open the frosted glass door, letting go of the handle when he reached above her head to hold the door open. The action sent her heart skipping faster than it already had been. "Thank you," she murmured.

"No problem."

She practically felt the smile on his face. When she turned to face him from the other side of her desk, smile confirmed.

"Please sit," she instructed as she sat.

She would have to find a way to forget the conversation they'd just had in the closet. Hell yes, she had something against him, but he couldn't know what it was. Then she'd have to admit to stalking him, which was not her thing. Toni was sure he'd had too many stalkers. His gigantic ego didn't need another. She placed the Styrofoam coffee cup on her desk. "Your office is right through that door." His gaze followed her pointing finger.

He showed her his profile as he glanced at the attached door. Good nose. And jaw. Sexy ears. Could ears be sexy? For God's sake. She sighed to herself. *I hate him.*

"I have to come in here to get to my office?" He turned to her, an eyebrow lifted.

"I'd rather you not cross through my office as you come and go. There is a door on the other side leading to a private copy room. You can get to the main corridor from there." She turned her gaze from his sun-filled eyes for a moment to glance at her phone. "I want you to use your intercom if you intend to come in my office."

Fabian's lips curled into an evocative smile, which she guessed was typical for his type. "I imagine, as your assistant, I'll be in your office a lot."

She shifted in her seat. "It is a possibility, yes."

He crossed an ankle over his knee, sinking in the chair that was obviously too small for his frame. "Oh, the possibilities…"

A glint danced in his eyes. He was toying with her. Trying to make her squirm, make her forget who was boss here. She had to snap out of it. In her mind she reread the letter Victor Pallis sent, feeling inspired to write him back now that she experienced what might amount to his son getting his way with women.

"What would be better is if you go through these invitations to galas, parties, openings, et cetera, and decide which events are the most beneficial for me to attend." She reached over, pulled out the second drawer of her massive desk and scooped up a load of envelopes with both hands. "I want a rationale for your decision to accept or decline for each one." She dumped the pile on the edge of the desk. A few fell over.

"This is what it means to be your assistant? Check your mail?" He didn't seem too amused with himself anymore.

"These events are important, Mr. Pallis. Robuchon Investments has a business standing and also a social standing in the community. If you are confused about either of those, I suggest you do some research." She was a little proud of herself for wiping that smirk off his face. Okay, she was a lot proud of herself.

He stood, scooping the envelopes with his large hands after he'd picked up the fallen ones. "As you wish, Miss Robuchon."

"Thank you."

When he slipped into the next room, she exhaled. God, dealing with him was harder than she thought it would be. She pulled up her email and selected the one from Victor Pallis. Again, she reread each word, grunting at the *he is used to getting his way with women* part. *Hell no. Not this woman.* She placed her fingers on the keyboard and typed as fast as she could.

To: Victor Pallis(Victor@PEngineering.biz)

From: Toni Robuchon(t.robuchon@robuchoninvestments.biz)

Date: Wednesday, July 13

RE:RE: Fabian

Mr. Pallis—I can assure you that Fabian will not receive any special treatment from myself or anyone on the Robuchon Investments staff. I fully read and understand your requirements, and I intend to fulfill your wishes. I find your approach estimable and smart. I am glad that my mother and I can help in your cause to reel in your loose cannon son. I can also assure you that Fabian will not get his way with any female employee at

Robuchon Investments in any capacity. We are a professional environment, and certain behaviors are looked down upon. These certain behaviors could potentially result in termination, and I am positive Fabian does not want that.

I will gladly report your son's progress on a weekly basis. I'm confident both parties—yourself and Robuchon Investments—will benefit from this arrangement.

P.S. Thank you for inquiring about my mother. She is on personal leave.

Sincerely,
Toni Robuchon
Acting CEO
Robuchon Investments
There. All done and sent. No turning back now.

Chapter Five

Fabian met his father for dinner that night at his favorite restaurant in Neartown around six-thirty. The restaurant served the best truffle lobster ravioli he'd ever tasted in the States. "Surprised you don't have one of your strippers with you." Fabian sipped from an old fashion glass filled with expensive scotch.

"She's not a stripper. And don't talk to me like that."

Fabian scoffed, not looking his father in the eyes. "Oh, sorry, adult entertainer."

"Fabian, you really should worry less about who I'm seeing and more about how you're going to prove to me you're responsible." His father shoved a pieced of rare tenderloin in his mouth. "You can't sustain the rest of your life with your tastes and what's left in your trust fund."

"How do you know that?"

"I know everything you do, boy."

Fabian cursed under his breath. God, he hated being called "boy". He was a man, and he had to keep his temper in check if he wanted to get anywhere with his dad. "I need to live, Dad. I need basic necessities."

"Like you needed a Flying Spur? You already have the Porsche and that Mercedes you never drive. Oh, that's right, you crashed the Mercedes on one of your drunken nights out with the guys."

"First of all, I wasn't drunk. I was trying to avoid another driver who ran a stoplight and ended up on the fire hydrant. And Bentley is a good car," he quipped. "You have one or five."

"Five that I bought with money I worked for."

"Is that what this is about? You're mad because I

spend the trust fund *you* set up for me? That seems ass-backward."

His father dropped his silverware on his plate. Fabian took in his father's glower, not saying another word. Their gazes fused brown to green. "This is about you wasting your life away. You're a Harvard grad, and you need to stop acting like a kid. Yes, you have a trust fund, but you need some…"

"Some what, Dad?"

"Pride in what you do. Purpose. You're a Pallis, and we've all been working men. *All of us*. Even me, and you know goddamn well I could have just bummed off my own trust fund." He rubbed the balding spot on his head. "And Antonia is right, I can't have you going around like a loose cannon. You're already in all the society papers with all your girlfriends, breaking hearts and causing scandals."

Fabian set down the heavy glass. "Wait, what? Loose cannon? Toni said that?"

"Yes, and I agree with her."

Fabian shifted in his seat, part exhilarated to know Toni was talking about him and part offended she would suggest such a thing. "When did she say that? And, by the way, you have no room to talk about all my girlfriends, Dad."

His father's thick eyebrow quirked up. "I have sense enough to stay out of the papers."

Before Fabian could respond, a man walked up to the table. Tall and blond, like he'd just come off a yacht. He slithered to them and placed a tanned hand on Fabian's father's shoulder. "Victor Pallis," the man greeted. He might have been in his late twenties. He looked very familiar to Fabian.

"Stephan! Nice to see you. Sorry to hear about that business deal. It was a big one," Fabian's father said.

Stephan nodded, stress stroked his eyes for only a moment. "Thank you, Victor. The Bradleys will prevail."

"No doubt. You know my son, Fabian."

"Right." Stephan nodded his head. After a quick wipe on his white pants, he offered a hand to Fabian. "You were thirteen the last time I saw you." Fabian took the hand, shook it with the same force Stephan put in. A competitive handshake would be the best way to describe it.

"Fabian was at Harvard for six years. Decided to grace Houston."

"I outgrew Cambridge," Fabian said, eyeing the white smile.

Stephan seemed impressed. "Both undergrad and grad, huh? Nice." He shoved his hand in his pocket. "You working with your old man now?"

Fabian's father cleared his throat, answering, "Not yet. He's assisting Robuchon for a while."

"Helene?" Stephan lifted both eyebrows, surprise taking residence in his clear blue eyes.

"Toni." Fabian tossed his father a curt glance.

"Antonia?" Stephan could barely contain himself. His mouth gaped a moment before he continued. "My Antonia? Ex-Antonia, I mean?"

My Antonia? Fabian suddenly became very interested. "What do you mean?"

"She's my ex-fiancée." He said it matter-of-fact with a tinge of threat. Blue eyes narrowed at Fabian as the two men gazed at each other.

"Is she?" A smirk curled his lips. Reaching for his drink, Fabian took a heady gulp, eyes still pinned to Stephan.

"Yeah, she is."

"Well, isn't that a coincidence?"

Fabian's father broke the awkward silence.

"Helene is on personal leave for a while, and Antonia is acting CEO. For now."

"That's odd." Stephan glanced down to his Richard Mille watch. Fabian would know it anywhere. The guy at least had good taste in watches. And women. "Good to run into you, Victor." He glanced to Fabian. "Fabian." And just as he turned, he said, "Tell Antonia I'll pay a visit tomorrow. Just to catch up."

Their gazes caught again, mingling. "I'll let her know." *Yeah, right.* No way in hell would he tell her. It would be too fun to watch her surprise at her ex-fiancé's visit. And hopefully distaste.

After Stephan was out of earshot, Fabian said, "He looks like a dick. Why would Toni be engaged to *that* guy?"

"She's not anymore," his father said around another mouthful of tenderloin.

Fabian continued to watch Stephan walk away until he'd blended into the crowded restaurant. He turned his attention back to his father. "What happened? With the engagement, I mean."

"Oh, you know. He cheated. Left her for someone else. Or something like that. Hell, I don't know."

To Fabian's surprise, his heart sank, and for a moment he felt somber. Men didn't cheat on women like Toni. Did they? She was probably perfect. Minus the icy exterior. After finding out about what happened to her engagement, he understood why she seemed so untrusting. She might even be a bit of a misandrist, which took him back to his previous question. "You never said when Toni called me a loose cannon."

"God, Fabian, let it go. You *are* a loose cannon."

"Yeah well, you're not exactly a straight arrow, Dad." Bad thing to say. He'd already been skating on thin ice since their last conversation.

"Watch yourself."

"Why would she even say that? What proof does she have to suggest I'm a loose cannon?" Misbehaving might be the worst she could accuse him of, but a loose cannon? That would need a lot more evidence, which validated his conclusion that she'd done some research on him.

"God, Fabian, you're my only son and I need you to be serious. Get your life together. And stop all the womanizing. Settle on one you can take as an acceptable wife from a good family. The kind of woman who is well connected. Like—"

"Like Antonia Robuchon," Fabian spit out, his heart pounding.

His father's eyebrows lifted and eyes narrowed. "No... I was going to say that Camille Carano girl you've been seeing. The Caranos are making a good name for themselves in the auto business." He stared at his son. Fabian knew exactly what he was thinking. "Now why would you assume I meant Antonia?"

Fabian planted his lips around the rim of the glass again, answering with a mumble. "She's connected."

His gaze caught his father's and held it. As the realization fell over Fabian's father's face, he nearly choked on the next piece of steak he'd stuffed in his mouth. "Oh, no. No way, son. You're not going to look or even think about Antonia in that way. She's off limits." He shook his head, his eyes growing wider with each demand. "I won't have you break her heart, too. I won't have you mess up my relationship with the Robuchons."

Fabian lifted his hands, shrugging his shoulders. "What do you mean?" The thought of him breaking Antonia's heart didn't sit well with him. "I wouldn't do that."

"No, Fabian. She is your boss, and off limits." He leaned in, over the small table. "You hear me? Off. Limits."

Fabian shrugged, playing it cool, though the butterflies fluttered in his stomach to think of Toni as an acceptable wife he could take. "No worries there, Dad. I don't think she likes me much anyway."

* * * *

Toni needed to decompress. Take all her stress out on her yoga mat, which is exactly what she did. The late class started at eight and at approximately nine-thirty she found herself standing outside the studio. She'd driven her Range Rover, wanting time to herself.

The thick, humid night air clung to her skin. She needed out of her clothes stat. On the hood of the SUV, she placed her mat before peeling off her t-shirt, gladly accepting the slight breeze, albeit warm, against the exposed skin around her sports top. She also took a long swig of vitamin water as she grabbed the mat again.

"It must be my lucky day." The voice startled her.

She knew exactly who it was. Fabian. The one person she didn't want to see. Rolling her eyes, she turned as she attempted to cover her bare stomach with her water bottle. "And clearly, I have bad timing."

How fast could she jump in the SUV and press the accelerator? Oh, God, had she really been planning her escape? This man cannot have that much influence over her. Fabian had taken off his bow tie and jacket. Her gaze wandered to his exposed forearms. Why did a man get a thousand percent more attractive with rolled up sleeves? Damn him. Still, her eyes moved down to his thick wrists and fingers. Gulping, she managed to lift her gaze back to his. He was oh-so-hot, standing in front of her with his hair a bit messy like he'd raked his fingers through it all evening. It made her want to run her fingers through his hair until morning. And then she reminded herself a ton of women had probably already done that.

"I forgot you live above my studio." *Pathetic lie. Need to get out of here.*

"I've got the sweetest pad in the whole building. You should see it sometime."

She didn't try to hide her eye roll. "I'll pass!"

He shrugged. "Suit yourself." Pivoting on his heels, he left her to gape after him.

Damn him!

By some force, she got herself together and into her SUV, her foot lying heavy on the accelerator. Adrenaline pumped through her body as she sped down Elgin Street. There went her Zen. Fabian had ruined her Zen twice. Given the chance, he might ruin other things for her too. She turned left on Montrose until she'd reached the underground garage of her high-rise residence.

Over and over, the conversation they'd just had played over her mind. *What an arrogant ass!* The man's nerve had no boundary. She should have fired him right on the spot for suggesting she see his "sweet pad". How many other women had he invited to his bachelor pad? And what about Camille Carano? Not that Toni cared about any of that. Especially Camille Carano. Or any other girlfriend. God, she couldn't stop obsessing. Toni wished she hadn't have sent Mary home. She needed a bubble bath and a cup of chamomile tea.

And she needed a man.

The last time a man had touched her was so long ago. Over a year ago. Though she was with Stephan, their intimacy had dwindled to nothing just before he ended the engagement. She'd been picking out flowers for their wedding reception and he was picking out a new girlfriend. *Sorry, babe, I'm just not into this anymore.*

That was what he'd said to her as she decided on peach roses for her bouquet. *What kind of a person says that? To your fiancée, no less?*

Her life had been bleak for the better of a year until she started her fake position at Robuchon Investments. But nothing was fake about it. The more time she sat in that executive chair, the more she started to believe she could actually be the CEO. The real CEO. One day. For now, she was going to prove herself as more than the trophy wife her mother always told her she would be.

In her living room, she tossed her rolled up mat on the 1920s fainting couch. Much of her apartment was decorated in art deco antiques. Toni fell on the pintucked wingback chair, sighing as she sank into it. Her gaze fell upon her fingers resting on her still bare stomach. She was sure she'd left a sweat stain on the delicate upholstery, but couldn't care in that moment. Fabian came to her again, filling her thoughts. A slight remembrance of him as a kid came to the forefront of her mind. Not the soccer one, though. He was walking with his dad somewhere. He wore jeans and a white polo shirt tucked in. How she remembered something so specific when she didn't remember much else was beyond her.

He seemed different then. Or maybe he wasn't. Perhaps everyone was different in childhood. By the time she returned to Houston from boarding school to enter Rice University as an undergrad, he was already at Harvard. Now here they were in the same city again.

A blast from her cell phone yanked her out of her thoughts. She jumped off the chair and raced to answer the ringing phone, noting it was her best friend from college, Melina Martin, calling.

"Hey, Mel!"

"Wow! I can't believe you answered." Melina's

voice rose a few octaves with her apparent surprise.

Toni sank on the couch, squeezing the mat as she spoke. "I know. I'm sorry about that. I've been out of pocket for a while."

"Try six months."

Had it really been that long since she'd spoken to her BFF? Toni did the math in her head. Yes, it had been six months. Last time they'd spoken was at a New Year's party. Stephan had shown up with the women he'd left Toni for. Needless to say it was disastrous, and Toni wanted to forget that event. "Wow."

"I thought you needed some space, which is why I didn't hound you. But, I've been worried about you. Are you okay? Rumor has it you took over your mom's position. Is that true?"

Her heart stilled. Toni didn't want to talk about her mother or her position. The position of being in chemotherapy for pancreatic cancer. She stuttered, "Yes, I did take over. Just temporarily, though."

"So, I have to ask you something else." Toni's insides knotted up. Had Melina found out about her mother? "Is it true that Fabian Pallis is your assistant?"

Not what Toni expected Mel to ask by her serious tone. Nothing about Fabian warranted a serious tone. "Where did you hear that?" Also, how could the rumor mill have started about his employment anyway? He'd just been hired for God's sake.

"A girl he is dating—I use that term loosely— goes to my Pilates class. Her name is Camille Carano. Do you know her?"

Ugh. Not that name again. Toni closed her eyes, pressing the space between them with her free index finger. A headache threatened to further ruin her night. "No, I don't know her. But I know of her."

"So … is it true then?"

She paused. Fabian was her employee now and she should get used to talking about it. "Yes, it's true. However, it's just a temporary thing until he goes to work for his dad."

Melina laughed. "That man is seriously hot! As in movie-star hot. As in I-might-consider-cheating-if-I-had-a-shot-with-him hot."

Toni tightened her lips. "I find him annoying and a bit rude, which detracts from any good looks he might have." She needed to get away from that topic. If she went on, she might admit she thought Fabian was movie star hot too. Refocusing, she continued, "Seriously, Mel, you would never cheat on a boyfriend if you had one. Wait, do you have one?"

"I know." She laughed. "And no, I don't."

Toni fought with herself not to say another word about Fabian. She failed miserably. "Fabian is also the cockiest man I've ever met."

"Yeah, what do you expect? He's just like every other hot, rich player in Houston."

Like Stephan. "True."

"Speaking of which, I heard Stephan cheated on that woman. Once a cheater, always a cheater, huh?" Mel always knew the current gossip. For better or worse.

A hot ripple ran through Toni at the sound of his name. She could have done without that information. "Stephan can go to hell. If I never see him again, it would be too soon."

Silence filled the receiver. "I know," Melina said. "You know what? Let's go out. Yeah, party it up like we did in college. It'll be fun."

"I'm pretty sure I didn't party it up, Melina." Toni laughed, remembering she didn't dare take a drink until she was exactly twenty-one. Following the rules was one of her strong points.

"Oh, right, that was me." She giggled. "Still, let's do something on Friday. A girl's night out downtown. H Bar is perfect for a little dancing and drinking. What do you say?"

A part of Toni wanted to, but the antisocial part didn't want to go out or meet new people. She actually wanted to work more on her proposal for the medical device company. Hesitating, she weighed her options. If she went, she'd at least get to chat with a good friend whom she hadn't seen in a while. And she'd be able to wear one of the many couture dresses hanging in her closet with the tags still dangling from them. What did she really have to lose? "Sure. Why not."

Melina squealed. "Yay! I'll pick you up at eight. We can get a drink somewhere beforehand."

"I'll have Miles drive us. We'll pick *you* up." Toni started to feel good about going. She was also sure they would need a chauffeur after all the drinks she intended to have.

Chapter Six

When Fabian walked in Antonia's office the next day, he caught her staring out the picturesque window, holding herself, completely unaware that he watched her. Head to foot, he admired her. Her dark hair was pulled back again into the high ponytail he liked. His gaze fell over the delicate curve of her neck, lingering there for a moment before he continued down to the rest of her body. Black cropped pants fit perfectly against her rounded ass. *Jesus.* He bit his bottom lip, thinking of all the things he wanted to do to that tight ass, and promptly feeling guilty for thinking those thoughts. The fact that he felt guilt about admiring an ass, which he'd done on many occasions, concerned him.

She turned, her dark eyes wide with surprise. "What are you doing?" Her gaze fell to the coffee cup in his grip. "Oh…"

He glanced at his watch. Eight-fifteen on the dot. "Your coffee, Miss Robuchon." A smile parted his face. She didn't smile back at him, though. What would it take to remove the permanent frown from her face?

"You didn't have to buy me a coffee…"

"I can afford it." He winked, and that only made her frown harder. "I also want to apologize for last night. I shouldn't have suggested you come up to my condo. That wasn't professional."

A sculpted eyebrow quirked up. She didn't believe him. "O-Okay…" A confused look crossed her face.

She took the coffee cup from his grip, her fingers brushing against his for a second. Though she pulled away, he chose to fixate on the sensation of her skin on his. She, on the other hand, acted as if there was no touch at all and lifted the cup lid to peer inside. She sniffed, making him laugh. Particular was the best way to describe her coffee tastes, which amused him.

"I promise it's organic milk," he said when she sniffed a second time and still didn't take a sip.

She glanced away then. At least her frown was gone. Then would have been the time to tell her about Stephan. But, he decided against it. All night he'd gone back and forth about it. Why it was such a big deal, he had no idea. He rationalized there wasn't an ethical issue with not telling her. In truth, the coffee was more than his duty as her assistant, it was his potential peace-offering for not telling her.

Finally, she sipped, a look of disdain creased her forehead when she removed the cup from her red lips. "This is *not* French roast!"

And that was why he didn't tell her about Stephan.

Icy, demanding, and entitled wouldn't win him over. She was entirely too damn beautiful to be acting that way. He grunted, pushing away the attraction he had for her before. None of it was his problem anyway. "I'm so glad you're as appreciative as I thought you'd be." He stepped toward his adjacent office.

She pressed her free hand to her tiny curving hip as if he was the issue, not her.

Liking her wasn't necessary, so he was grateful she acted like a complete brat. His father said she was off limits, and she was doing a great job keeping him at bay. If she kept up that crappy attitude, his only mission would be to get the hell out of RI as fast as he could. Without looking back at her, Fabian strode to his office. He hoped she watched him leave.

Waiting in his office was the stack of invitations he needed to go through. He shook his head at the pile of envelopes, feeling like a complete chump. *I'm going to kill my dad.* RSVPing to invitations was not a job for a person who'd graduated from Harvard—twice. He sighed, sitting at his desk, picking up the first envelope. The first was the Museum of Fine Arts gala and silent auction. Every year Pallis Engineering had contributed a sizable amount to the event. Pallis Engineering also always sponsored a private dinner beforehand.

As he worked through the invitations, he'd come across a manila folder labeled NeuRx Proposal. With interest, he opened the folder and scanned the pages inside. An executive order had been stamped *Denied*, though a sticky note adhered to the sheet read *Do More Research.* It might have been Toni's handwriting. It also said, in neat cursive *What Do I Know?* Next to it was a question mark and a sad face. This compelled him to continue to read more.

After reading through Toni's file on neurostimulation technology for ten minutes, he researched the startup requesting funding for a clinical study. He hadn't used his bioengineering skills since undergrad, but he'd understood everything as if he was a working engineer. About an hour later, he closed the manila folder. His gaze moved over to the wall. Toni had something. More than that, she had something really good. Why had the execs denied NeuRx? Despite his petty differences with Toni, he completely agreed with her assessment.

With a tight grip on the folder, he crossed into Toni's office. "Hey—"

"Excuse me." She looked up from her desk, annoyed with the intrusion. "You're supposed to use the intercom if you want to come in my office."

He was taken aback. "Are you serious?"

Eyebrows rose to the middle of her forehead.

"Um, yeah. Dead serious." They were now reduced to siblings going at it so easily.

He clenched his jaw, careful to contain himself. "Okay, but, I'm here now. I'll remember for next time. Okay?"

"What is it?" She leaned back in her chair, both arms crossing over her chest.

"This." He put the folder on her desk.

Her eyes grew wide at the sight. She scanned her desk as if she'd lost something. "Where did you get that?"

"It was with the invitations you asked me to review. I guess took it by mistake."

She snatched the folder, quickly slipping it in her desk drawer. "Thanks for giving it back." Her gaze fell to her desk as she shuffled around papers and irrelevant things in obvious attempt to avoid his eyes. Still not looking at his, she asked, "Have you looked at the invitations?"

Perplexed as he was about her reaction, he pressed on regardless. "I think NeuRx is a good investment too."

Their gazes met. Her eyes had softened to something he'd not recognized in her. She'd always been hard to connect with up until that point. "You read my proposal notes?"

The uncertainty in her eyes was disconcerting to him because all she'd ever been since he'd met her was completely sure of herself. He nodded, his tone softer. "Yeah, I did. I think what you said about users wanting a product with longer battery life is spot on. There's nothing else exactly like it on the market now. I don't understand why the executive team denied it."

Glossy eyes stared back at him and for a moment he thought she would cry. He even braced himself for the waterworks, which wasn't something he liked dealing with. Women's tears made him run for the hills. Every time. She didn't, though.

Toni shrugged, her voice deeper when she spoke. "None of them are bioengineers." Something else happened that he thought she'd never do in regards to him. She smiled. But it all faded too fast. Her frown emerged. "This was private, Mr. Pallis. I wish you hadn't pried."

Completely stunned at the change of pace, he hesitated, looking for the right words. He found none. *"Okay..."*

By then her wall was up again and he knew he wouldn't be able to reach her. Without bothering to look at him, she said, "I appreciate your assessment."

"Anytime." They were done. Fabian didn't know how to reach her again. He'd gotten a glimpse of her soft side, and hated that it went away so fast. How could be bring it back? He simply had to figure out a way. "I can help you with the technology part of the proposal. I understand how it's supposed to work."

No response. Their conversation about the proposal was over. "Any updates on the invitations?"

Nice, soft Toni was gone. He rubbed the back of his neck. "The Museum of Fine Arts gala is a definite RSVP. Pallis Engineering is holding a private sponsors dinner. I think this would look favorable for RI."

"Oh, right. We do like that event. Is it too late to be a sponsor?"

"It might be closed, but I'm sure we can pull some strings. I know the person in charge." He winked, trying to get things lighter again between them. In turn, she gifted him with an eye roll. They were at their baseline of communication. Still, an awkward silence expanded between them, giving him the perfect opportunity to change subject back to the proposal, despite his knowing he needed to let it go. "Hey, I didn't mean to pry by reading your proposal. I just thought it was really good. You're extremely smart."

"And you don't think women can be smart, Mr. Pallis?" she snapped, glowering at him.

"No, I didn't say that at all—"

"You pissing off my girl, Pallis?" The voice came from the other side of the room, interrupting him. Both Fabian and Toni turned their attention to Stephan Bradley standing at the door.

* * * *

Toni blinked once, and then a second time to make sure she was seeing properly. "What the hell are *you* doing here?" In effort to sound angry, she ended up sounding winded.

Her heart raced as realization sank in. Stephan was in her office. The cheating bastard she'd once wanted to marry more than anything else was in her office.

"Didn't your secretary tell you I was coming today?" Stephan glanced at Fabian, his lips curled up in a smirk.

"I'm not a damn secretary," Fabian barked, his jaw clenching.

"Did you know about his?" She stared at Fabian, her blood was boiling. How dare he keep that information from her!

Stephan interjected, "Last night I saw old man Pallis and Fabian at Hugo's. I told him I would come by for a chat." His sparkling blue eyes turned to Fabian. "You didn't tell her, man? Not cool, bro."

"I'm not your bro or your messenger." Fabian's lips pressed together. Why was Fabian so angry? Toni suspected there was more to the story, but she couldn't get passed Fabian keeping this information from her.

Toni pinned Fabian's stare in place, her heart pounding faster with each second. "But you're *my* assistant, Fabian."

"In business matters, not personal." He had her there. Still, why wouldn't he give her a heads-up? The deliberate withholding made her furious. What was even more infuriating was watching Fabian turn to walk back to his office without another word. She clenched her fists as the sound of the closing door echoed through her office.

Dear God, how was she supposed to deal with Stephan alone? As ridiculous as it sounded, she wanted Fabian back for protection. She glanced at the picturesque window, wondering if there was an escape route from that high up. Jumping out of the window was more appealing to her than saying another word to him. She hadn't anticipated ever seeing Stephan again, in person anyway. They hadn't as much as bumped into each other since the New Year's disaster.

"Someone has a crush on you," Stephan teased, moving his large athletic body deeper into the office.

She jerked around to face him. "That's absurd."

Before she could position herself to be on the offense, he was in her personal space, touching her shoulder with thick tan fingers. "What's absurd is that I haven't talked to you in way too long."

His touch singed her skin and not in a good way. "It hasn't been that long. I could go longer."

He laughed that same smooth laugh she used to love. *Used* to. "You know, this weekend would have been our wedding. Do you ever think about that?"

She turned away. She vowed never to show emotion in front of him ever again. He didn't deserve that from her. "No."

"Come on, baby. I know you do." He grabbed her

hand, lifting it to his lips. The kiss he pressed on her palm shot waves through her body. But they weren't waves that made her stomach flutter. They made her want to vomit. "You're still so beautiful."

She pulled her hand away and managed to find the strength in her voice. "What do you want, Stephan?"

He was far too close to her, looking at her like he wanted to eat her alive. Blue eyes adjusted as he examined her face, his eyes zeroing in on her mouth. This man knew no boundaries. Clearly, he thought he still had the right to be so close to her. Pompous ass. Just when she thought he'd crossed the line, he bent over her, caging her in with both hands on the arms of her executive chair. He breathed in deep, moaning as he did it. "I miss you."

"What about Sarah?" *Ugh. Why did I say that?* She hated herself even more for not only engaging him but showing him how much he'd hurt her. Looking at him, she wondered how she ever loved him.

Somehow he got closer, his warm breath covering her face. "She was never you. Could never be you."

A lumped formed at the base of her throat. She wanted to faint. She was hot with his body so close and suffocating from his presence. She wished he'd stayed away. Why would he come and stir up old emotions? What a cruel game he played. The more she thought about it, the angrier she got. *Hell no*. He wasn't allowed to waltz in and tell her such things after he'd broken her heart to pieces—pulverized her. "Get away from me." It was a strong whisper. She pushed him away.

He took a step back. Still not enough, though. Out of her office would be better. His forehead creased with the turn of events, which probably wasn't what he was expecting, knowing him. Not too sure of himself now it would seem. Finally, she'd had the upper hand for once.

"I know it's a lot to hear. After everything. After I—"

"Dumped me for another woman as I was planning our wedding." Her spine straightened.

"Please don't say that, love. It sounds so harsh." What a low blow to call her "love", the pet name he'd given her.

She stood on shaky legs, determined to exert her power. "You need to go."

"I know you're caught off guard. But had your assistant told you about my visit, you'd have time to prepare."

What! She would explode at any moment if he continued. "To prepare? Are kidding me, Stephan?" Fabian was going to hear about this. God, she wished she could fire his ass for not telling her. "No." She shook her head, circumventing Stephan to the door. "I want you to leave now."

"Can't we talk?" he pleaded, which was odd to hear. And very satisfying. The tables had turned. In wide steps, he met her at the door, towering over her. "I want you to think about forgiving me. I want to try us again. Dumping you was the dumbest thing I've ever done."

Dumping you?

One. Two. Three. She needed to contain herself. Forgiving Stephan would never happen. Ever. This visit solidified her decision despite how emotionally drained she felt. "I will never forgive you."

The room was eerily silent. Only the faint buzz of her laptop sounded within the space. Because he didn't know how to be rejected, he brought a finger to her cheek, disregarding what she had just said. "Let me take you to dinner. Let me make it up to you."

She pushed his finger away. "You can never make it up to me."

A grin parted his face. "I take that as a challenge."

"Go." She choked on the single word, hating herself for showing more emotion. He didn't deserve that from her.

When he was gone, she exhaled the largest breath on the planet. The anger inside her put motion to her feet. In rapid speed—the fastest she could travel in her four-inch-heeled pumps—she found herself at Fabian's office door. Not hesitating, she pounded on the door with a tight fist several times.

"Fabian!" When he didn't respond, she opened the door. No Fabian. She sighed with a surprising relief. Seeing her irrational was a terrible idea. He already thought she was emotional anyway by the way she'd reacted to his reading her proposal, she surmised. A cup of coffee with a sticky note on the handle grabbed her attention. Her name was spelled out in all cap letters. She walked over and lifted it.

I promise this is French roast. I thought you might need it.
—F

Chapter Seven

On Friday morning while Fabian dressed for work, he couldn't erase what happened the day before out of his mind. Toni had an issue with compliments. Or it was just his compliments that were the issue? He honestly thought it was the former. He frowned at himself in the mirror. Didn't she believe she was smart? Fabian frowned harder, remembering her ex interrupting them just when Fabian thought he and Toni could actually have a normal conversation. The whole situation had left him reeling and dissecting his feeling all night and morning. Would he ever get a glimpse of soft Toni again?

At the office, Fabian noted that Toni's door was closed. Maybe she hadn't arrived, but it was already five past eight. He walked to the break room to see Davina standing at the coffee machine brewing a new carafe. He nodded, too distracted to notice her outfit. "Hey." He turned his gaze to the refrigerator, hoping there was organic milk in there.

"Going to try your hand at Toni's special coffee?" She laughed. Fabian didn't.

He strode to the refrigerator, pulling the handle. "I really hope there is organic milk in here."

"We're fresh out."

"Shit," he muttered. Two choices wrangled in his brain. Tell her the coffee was prepared with organic milk and hope she would believe him. Or, go buy organic milk, which would put her first sip in the eight-thirty timeframe. He sighed, closing the stainless steel door.

"I've snuck regular milk in her coffee before. She didn't know the difference."

Fabian stared at Davina, appalled at what she'd said. It didn't matter if it was about milk or not. Lying would be a complete breach of trust. He waited, hoping Davina would say she wasn't serious. Nope, she was serious. He shook his head. The silly milk dilemma suddenly seemed not so silly. "She'll know it's not organic."

Davina shrugged. "She shouldn't be so picky anyway."

Two days ago he would have agreed. That morning, he felt differently about her coffee and her. It was perplexing. "See ya," he said over his shoulder, catching a glimpse of Davina's frown as he departed.

The hall to Toni's office seemed longer than usual. With each stride, he grew increasingly nervous, glancing at his watch multiple times. *Almost eight-fifteen.* And just as he was about to turn the doorknob to her office, she yanked it open from the other side. He jumped back, his pulse racing. Damn, she was stunning in that black suit. Her hair was pulled up in a bun on top of her head. Somehow, he managed to speak. "There's no organic milk."

"Mr. Pallis, you're late. And of all the days I really need my coffee this morning." She clutched her manila folder against her chest. "The weekly execs meeting is in fifteen minutes." She sighed heavily and turned on her black heels back inside her office. He followed.

"I didn't know, Toni." He forgot himself for a moment while admiring her body in her tailored suit. "I mean, Miss Robuchon."

"Just forget it. I have to prepare." She sat in a slump. Had she come out of her office to find him? He liked that idea. Without looking up, she said, "You can leave now."

"Are you going to present your proposal for NeuRx?" He didn't want to leave yet.

Annoyed, she faced him. It was one of those days for her. The fact that she answered surprised him. "Yes, I am. I'm going to make a fool of myself again and hear *again* how I'm inexperienced and don't know anything about investing. Not that it's any of your business."

"They said that to you?" He felt warm, hot even, with the information.

She shrugged, looking down again at her folder. "They're right. I don't have work experience."

So that was defeatist Toni. He wasn't sure how to take it. Though he first felt angry at the executives. "The proposal is solid."

"Just get out, Fabian." She waved him away. "I don't need a pep talk. Not from you anyway. You don't have work experience either."

Cold Toni emerged. Inside he started to feel cold Toni was just a front. But he was getting tired of her being rude when he only wanted to help.

"I'm not trying to pep talk you. Why the hell would I do that? I don't care if you present or not. It's on you if you think they're right. I will say I hope you have a more positive attitude when you do present, though." He wanted to turn from her, walk out and not give a shit about her organic milk.

"I really don't need this, Pallis." The way she said his last name excited him. They stared at each other, energy swirling around them. "It's enough that those execs and my own mother don't think I can do this job."

"So prove them wrong." A concept he was getting cozy with, especially in regards to his father.

She shook her head, a sigh escaping her. Turmoil darkened her eyes. He knew exactly what she was going through. "I just ... nothing. Forget it." She averted her gaze to her manila folder again.

The urge to save her from the executives drove

him to form an idea that sent him walking until he passed through the front door of Robuchon Investments.

* * * *

Toni sat in the largest conference room staring at the CFO, COO, CIO and a handful of vice presidents that kept Robuchon Investments afloat. They were all men, except the vice president of investment analysis who might as well have been a man by her cutthroat attitude. Because men were cutthroat. At least, that was Toni's belief since her father passed away ten years ago. He was the last kind man she'd ever known.

She glanced at the clock ticking on the wall in the silence. "Is everyone ready to start the meeting?" All eyes were on her, and none of them looked impressed or interested. Bored was the best description. Maybe even loathing.

The COO, Mark Brand, rolled his eyes, as he usually did when Toni opened her mouth. "I have yet to hear from your mother. Can you update us on her personal leave?"

Translation—when are you leaving?

Toni glanced at the faces looking at her, waiting for her to speak. But the lump in her throat rendered her silent. Keeping her mother's condition a secret was way harder than she thought it would be. "My mother is still on leave."

"We got that. Do you know when she will return?" The COO's condescending tone prickled Toni's skin. And the way he looked up at her from over his reading glasses. She wanted to hurl her coffee at him, if she had it. Damn Fabian.

"No, Mr. Brand. Not at this time." The executives sighed in unison.

"So you don't know anything? I find that hard to believe, since you are ... her daughter." The COO didn't let up, and the rest of them egged him on. When several seconds passed and she didn't respond, he asked in his typical rude tone, "Antonia, did you hear what I asked?"

"Uh…" Speak or leave the room? Those were her choices. She wanted to leave the room. Her whole body contracted for a quick departure just when the door to the room swung open and Fabian entered, carrying two coffee holders stuffed with eight tall cups from Starbucks.

"Sorry for the interruption, but I wanted to bring coffees for the meeting. I apologize for being five minutes late." He set the holders down, taking one cup in his hand. The group seemed pleased and not annoyed as Toni was.

He walked over to her, handing over the cup. "French roast, organic milk, and three packets of cane sugar just for you, Miss Robuchon."

"I…" Toni didn't know what to say or do. She didn't even offer a smile for what he did. The cup was still hot, and when she dipped her face to sip, she felt his eyes on her. Finally, she said, "You didn't have to do this."

"Probably not." He beamed. How annoying. But, as much as she hated to admit it, it was a sweet gesture. His generosity gave her pause. Made her reconsider some of her preconceived notions of him. Not all, though. He was still a playboy. Nothing could possibly change her mind about that.

"This is my new executive assistant, Fabian Pallis. My mother hired him," Toni announced to the executives. They smiled at him with glee. Apparently, any mention of her mother was a good thing.

With Fabian still in the room, Mr. Brand addressed the group. "Do we have any investment potentials this week?"

Toni froze, her fingers wrapped around her folder. Her heart pounded so hard, she wasn't sure if caffeine was a good idea. The air grew hot all of a sudden and if she threw up that might be the best way out of the meeting. She sensed Fabian watching her. How could she look up at him after their conversation not even half an hour ago? Oh, God. She'd never been so nervous in her life.

"Sorry to interrupt again…"

Oh, God, no.

Fabian continued, "But Miss Robuchon has new information on the NeuRx technology that is riveting."

Riveting? Toni wanted to kill him.

Toni snapped her eyes to Fabian, hoping he saw the threat in her look. She also hoped that he knew he was done. Fired. No questions asked. He would be packing his bags, and she wouldn't care one bit if it would ruin his chances to work at his family firm.

Could she really do that? No…

The vice president of investment analysis spoke up. "We've rejected that proposal."

Toni cleared her throat, still boring her stare into Fabian, who looked like he knew he'd messed up royally. "I've consulted with a bioengineer on the technology, and I believe it has merit. If you can just take a look at the update—"

Mr. Brand shook his head. "No, we've all agreed. Your mother included. We won't revisit that proposal." He sipped his cup nonchalantly. A bit too smug. Toni knew he wanted to be CEO, at least that's what the rumors were. But RI had never employed a non-family CEO.

"Except, Mr. Brand, I don't feel the initial proposal described the technology and user needs effectively since no one on our team is a degreed bioengineer."

A few of the executives laughed.

Mr. Brand spoke for the team, his condescending tone raised a notch. "We understood it fine, Antonia. And we rejected it."

"If you can look at Miss Robuchon's notes—"

"That's all, Mr. Pallis, thank you," Toni snapped. Did he never shut up? The man was completely out of control. She was right to call him a loose cannon.

Fabian had the nerve to shrug before he left her to the wolves. Her anger reached an all-time high with him. Screw the coffee. He crossed the line and he certainly would hear about it.

After the unsuccessful meeting, Toni stomped down the hall to her office with her manila folder tight in her grip. Once she was in her office, she threw down the folder and punched the intercom button on her phone. "Fabian, get in here. Now." She hung up without waiting for his response.

He came in, hair messy like he'd been rubbing it the last hour. But his nonchalance irked her to the core. His lips curled up. "Yes?"

Her face burned. "Really?"

His eyes narrowed. "You seem upset."

"Hell yes, I'm upset!" She needed to pause a second or else she might lunge at him, literally kill this man who looked at her like *she* did something wrong. "You embarrassed me in front of the execs."

He frowned. "That one guy was a complete asshole."

She lifted her hands in the air. "Yeah, he is. But what you did was unforgivable." She pointed her finger, waved it around as she continued her tirade. "You will never go into an executive meeting again. Do you hear me? Or else, I don't care what arrangement our parents have, I will fire you so fast."

He lifted his own hands. "Fine." She really hated how hot he looked when he was surrendering. "I was just trying to help. I thought you needed it."

"Well, I don't." A complete lie. But she walked over to her desk, pulled out the ridiculously large executive chair and sat, still shaking. She hated how conflicted she was about Fabian. He really did help her, sort of. At least she knew his intention was genuine. He'd also brought her coffee, just like she liked it. But she didn't want to like him damn it. Toni managed to contain herself. "You can leave now."

"I'm not trying to make you look like an idiot, you know. I can tell this is hard for you, for whatever reason." She waved him away until he left her. The look in his eyes was too much. He didn't know anything about her. Not even a clue. Better to keep him at a distance.

Chapter Eight

Fabian's cell phone beeped under the blankets. *Camille*. She'd called him multiple times throughout the afternoon. Some women were so damn persistent.

He wasn't in the mood to talk to her, especially when all he could do was obsess about Toni and their latest heart-to-heart. He'd never met a person that was so insistent on refusing help. Did she think he was just messing with her? Clearly she thought his generosity was a joke. It wasn't. But worse than that, she thought he was a joke. He hated that. A joke was the last thing he wanted to be to her. If only she could see they had a lot more in common than she assumed. The executives treated her much like his own father treated him every time they spoke. Fabian knew what it was like to be talked down to. To not have the respect of someone you wanted respect from. The thought sent him back to the conversation he'd had with his dad at Hugo's.

Take a wife who's connected.

Fabian's mother had been a Swedish maid, not socially connected at all. She had worked for his grandfather. Fabian mused about his mother. Life must have been hard for her. He felt the ache of abandonment in his bones when he thought of his mother leaving. His father was a hard man to love. Fabian imagined neither had a chance of happiness in his parents' scenario. If only he'd known his mother, grown up with her, things might have been different for him. She could have taught him how to treat a woman properly before he entered into the dating scene. His father clearly didn't have a clue, so Fabian had to guess at just about everything women related.

His cell phone buzzed again, yanking him from

his reverie. *Argh*. His heart pounded as he reached for the phone. Not Camille. His oldest friend, Tylund Westmore's face flashed on the screen. Thank God. His being an asshole quota had been reached for the day. Still, he knew he'd have to talk to Camille eventually. Sooner rather than later. He'd rather talk to Ty anyway. "Hey man."

"What's up, bro? You game for tonight?" Ty's voice was husky from sleep. A night of debauchery most likely kept in him bed the whole day.

"What's going on tonight?" Fabian checked his watch. Fifteen until seven.

"The crew is doing a guy's night of boozing and womanizing." No big deal.

"What we do best." Fabian would have laughed at the statement before, but something about it was no longer funny. Or appealing.

"Precisely. Plus, I want to take out the new Ferrari."

"Oh, you got it?"

"My driver picked it up this morning." Completely normal behavior. Good thing Ty didn't have the stress of a father who wanted him to find a purpose or else he might actually have to wake up in the morning.

"Sweet!" Fabian rubbed his chin stubble. "What's on the itinerary?"

"Drinks at your place in an hour. Then some dinner at Smith and Wollensky. More drinks at H Bar. My buddy, Frank, is deejaying tonight. Got a table— bottle service. You know how we do it."

"Indeed, I do." Fabian smiled. A guy's night is exactly what he needed to end the what seemed like a never-ending week. He could've sworn he'd already been working at RI for a month.

"And then whatever the hell else we single, red-blooded males want to do." Ty grew louder. He was the kind of guy who always motivated the group. He was a football player in school. Probably could have made it to the NFL if he really tried. But he was just a lazy son of a bitch, which worked well with having a trust fund.

"As long as you assholes keep your clothes on, I'm game for whatever. I'm not trying to see your pencil dicks, though."

"Whatever, dude. I'm well-hung. *Well*." Ty's famous line.

Fabian chuckled. "I'm just going to take your word for it." The next question wasn't premeditated. It should have been, because he regretted it immediately. "Do you know Antonia Robuchon?"

A slow response came after a long pause. "Yeah … I know Toni. Why?"

"I'm her assistant." *Shut the hell up, Pallis.* Fabian hadn't planned on telling any of his friends about the job. He'd figured he wouldn't be there long enough. Now, he would never hear the end of it.

A booming laugh filled the receiver, and it didn't stop. A full minute later when Fabian thought Ty had gotten his fill, the laugh continued. Harder. "*What!* Why the hell are you her assistant? I mean, is old man Pallis out of business or what?" A couple of lighter chuckles followed.

"My dad wants me to work for Helene Robuchon before he makes me partner. Apparently, I have to prove I'm responsible or some shit." The explanation was flippant, but Fabian knew there was merit to it. As much as he hated to admit it.

"For how long?" Ty sounded like himself again—less of a sarcastic asshole.

"Not long. Helene had to go on leave and Toni stepped in her place and that's why I'm working for her instead."

"No shit?" Ty's reaction was what probably everyone's was. Amazed. "Little T is seriously the CEO of Robuchon Investments?"

"Seriously."

"Congrats, my friend. Talk about an ugly duckling turning into a swan. She's hot. Anti-social, but hella hot. I'm a little envious." He continued, "She was with that jackass Stephan Bradley all through college and grad school."

Fabian tensed at the mention of Stephan's name. Stephan Bradley was a class A asshole. Why would she slum with the likes of him? Fabian would never understand that. Good thing he was away and didn't have to witness that relationship go south. "I missed a lot being Cambridge for six years."

"She was in our private school. Remember?"

Fabian strained at the memories of his youth. Found them troubling sometimes. He kept some memories, and was glad to forget the others. "Yeah, sort of. She didn't exactly stand out."

He laughed. "No, she didn't. But when she came back from Georgia, she was like a new woman. "

"Are you friends with her? You've never talked about her to me."

"No, we're not friends. More like social acquaintances. My mom brunches with Helene, though, a couple times a year. A charity thing I guess. I should ask her on a date. Show her a good time, you know."

Fabian laughed, though he wanted to claim her. How stupid is that? Rationality aside, his instinct was to call dibs on her. "Dude, you wouldn't have a chance with her."

"Neither would you." Ty laughed but it came to stuttered stop quickly. The silence spoke volumes. Of course Ty read between the lines. Why couldn't he be lazy *and* dumb? Dumb he definitely was not. "Hold up. Are you trying to date her?"

"*No*." Fabian walked toward his picturesque window to look over the still bright sky even though it was evening. He needed to refocus. No was not the right answer. His stomach flopped with the lie he told his friend—and himself. "Besides I don't need to try. Panties drop when I step in a room."

"Indeed!" Ty laughed. God, Fabian really hated himself then. Ty continued, "So tonight. Drinks will be had. And panties will be dropped."

* * * *

"Oh, my God! That dress is like … wow!" Melina pulled Toni into her small apartment, garnering a closer look at Toni's dress.

Melina didn't have a trust fund like most of Toni's friends, or acquaintances rather. Mel was from a lower middle-class family who lived in a run-down neighborhood in southwest Houston. Academically, Melina was über smart. Ridiculously. Enough to go to Harvard Medical School. But Melina was also social, so she chose to have a life instead of study medicine. She did well as a chemical engineer at an oil and gas company. Toni met Melina at Rice University, where they'd been roommates for a semester until Toni decided dorm life wasn't for her. She promptly moved into one of the family's museum district penthouses for the other semesters, which is where she remained. She'd offered one of the four bedrooms in the penthouse to Melina, but she'd declined. Making it on her own was important to Melina. Toni always admired her for that.

"But look at you!" Toni pointed at Melina's outfit. Knockout was the only way to describe her. Tall with an hourglass figure, she looked great in lingerie and bikinis. Toni always felt a little inadequate when she stood next to her, being on the petite side. She tilted her head, continuing her admiration. "You're a walking Agent Provocateur ad. Seriously. Bravo, beautiful!"

Melina's light brown hair was styled in a deep side part and pin-straight, kissing her collarbone. Her black bandage dress was reminiscent of a dominatrix outfit, as were the tall multi-strapped heels adorning her feet. Melina ran her palms down the front of her dress. "This is what you call an Express clearance special." She laughed, turning her attention to Toni's dress again. "Yours is straight from the runway and probably never goes on clearance."

True. The dress was right off the runway. Literally. Most of Toni's dresses were. Funny how that never really occurred to her until it was pointed out. She frowned, thinking on it as she stared at Melina. "Want to trade?" She took Melina by her hipbones until their stomachs touched.

Melina smiled, a short-lived well of emotion in her eyes. She placed her hands over each of Toni's. "I'm so happy to see you, friend."

"I'm happy to see you, too." They hugged. A knot formed in Toni's throat. She would cry if she didn't worry about ruining her mascara. But being there with Melina moved something inside her. She felt like she could relax and not worry about being anything but who she was. Melina was the only person who understood her.

When they parted, Melina wiped the black tear tracks from her eyes. She turned toward the kitchen. "A cocktail before we go?"

"Absolutely." Toni needed to lift herself from the sadness that had been hanging over since her mother's secret diagnosis. How would she keep it from her dearest friend? It had been hard enough to keep it from people who weren't that dear to her.

In the kitchen, Melina opened the refrigerator, surveying the contents. Not much to choose from what Toni could tell, peering over her shoulder.

Melina turned back to Toni, eyebrows lifted. "How about a screwdriver?" She took out a bottle of vodka from the freezer. She turned, both hands wrapped around bottles. "Tito's Vodka and organic orange juice. What's better than that?"

Toni smiled, taking in her friend's enthusiasm. Nothing. Nothing was better than that. "Sounds perfect."

They drank a total of three-and-a-half screwdrivers before loading into the Robuchon limo. "I cooled the Krug, Miss Robuchon," Miles said before he rolled up the privacy window.

"Krug!" Mel squealed, obviously tipsy. Toni was quickly approaching her cut-off point, but it was girl's night and it had been too long since they hung out. If they drank a bit too much, too bad. Toni would accept the consequences in the morning. Thank God for Miles.

"We should slow down." Toni pulled the smoking bottle from the ice bucket.

Mel fell against the leather seat. "I know. We should." She dragged a hand over her face. "At this rate, I'll be passed out before we make it to H Bar." She laughed as she closed her eyes, but not before accepting the champagne flute Toni handed her.

"Just sip a little." Toni fell back into the seat with her own flute, taking small sips of the popping liquid. Under the influence, Toni wanted to tell Melina about everything that had happened that week. Stephan's visit. Her mother's diagnosis. Fabian. Oh, God, Fabian. She sipped more instead.

"How goes it with hot muffin?" Melina asked as if she'd read Toni's mind.

"Huh?" Toni sipped again, longer that time. If she kept sipping, she physically wouldn't be able to talk about hot muffin. *Hot muffin?*

Melina narrowed her eyes and took a long sip. "That's cute."

Toni straightened up. "What?" Toni averted her eyes, releasing her breath. *Should I tell her?* She struggled with the dilemma, knowing if she didn't tell someone, she might explode. "Fine. I know you're talking about Fabian. And I'm in no condition to talk about him."

Melina eyes were intense on Toni. The woman was too damn good at picking out her secrets just by looking at her. Always had been. Maybe that was part of the reason why she stayed away for so long after the New Year's Eve debacle.

Melina started off slow. "You know … I'm not sure he's with Camille anymore."

Toni's heart roared between her ears. Her whole body tingled. Damn champagne. "Yeah. So…"

"So I heard Camille tell someone in Pilates class this morning that he was ignoring her calls."

Ignoring her calls? Toni pushed what that suggested away from her mind. Staying rational would be the challenge. She contained herself, trying to show no emotion about Fabian. "And…"

"And you sure are trying to avoid any conversation about him too hard." Melina touched her leg to force her attention. "Why is that, Toni Robuchon?"

She sighed. "I'm not trying to avoid the conversation about him, I just don't have anything to say besides what I already did."

"Which is…"

"He's a complete ass." Of course Toni failed to mention all the bitchy things she did to him, which were a lot. The coffee incident came to mind. She really should apologize. Or not.

"I don't remember you saying complete ass."

Toni waved the flute around, spilling champagne on the seat. "What are you, some kind of a…" She couldn't find the words. "Some kind of remembering police?" *Ugh.*

Melina laughed. "No. But I am the I know-when-my-friend-likes-someone police. And it's okay to like someone, Toni."

Melina put her lips on the rim of the flute, lingering there.

Her stare pinned Toni through her core. She felt completely naked, and couldn't find a response. She hadn't allowed herself to like anyone in a long time. Wasn't about to start now.

Melina shook her head. Apparently, she had her all figured out. "You like him. In fact, you like him a lot. I *know* you want to have his Pallis Greek babies!" She laughed wildly, nudging Toni's foot with her own.

Toni rolled her eyes and looked out the window at the highway signs for downtown. They'd soon approach the exit to H Bar. "I would never punish my offspring that way."

Melina laughed. "Seriously! Be serious. You've spent this whole week at work with him and there's nothing to say?"

The meeting came to mind. What she said. What he said. It all came back. And she wanted to repeat what she'd said minutes ago—he's a complete ass. But after what had transpired—his concerned gaze when she confessed her insecurity and his surprise coffee run for the executives—she really couldn't say he was a complete anything. Besides him being a playboy because nothing had changed her mind about that. But she'd connected with him and it scared her. Not that Melina needed to know about that.

Toni grabbed the Krug bottle from the ice bucket and poured a bit into each flute. She lifted her glass, and said, "Cheers to girls' night out."

Melina took her glass away, mock disdain on her face. "No way, sister. You better not evade the question."

"Okay fine." Toni had to give Melina something to chew on, or else she'd never hear the end of it. So, she went with the truth. "He's a terrible assistant. But at least he looks good."

"Cheers to that!"

Chapter Nine

Fabian savored the twenty-five-year-old scotch on this tongue before he swallowed. Only special patrons at H Bar had access to the good liquor. The bottle probably cost as much as someone's rent. Screw his dad. Fabian went all out when he partied. Tonight he was in a partying mood.

"My old man drinks that shit," Ty shouted from the other side of the low table between two couches in the VIP section. His blue eyes glittered from the track lighting overhead in the VIP nook. They had a perfect view of the dance floor and the DJ booth. Everyone on the other side were no doubt envious of their seating. No one could get that nook without the owner's invitation.

Fabian swallowed another measured gulp, pointing at Ty's drink. "And my old man's stripper girlfriend drinks what you're having!"

Another childhood friend, Dallas Halman, laughed as if it was the funniest thing he'd heard all day. He'd been tipsy since dinner. He pushed Ty's arm, spilling the vodka and cranberry juice on his jeans.

"Fucker!" Ty gazed down at his lap. Setting down the drink, he met Fabian's gaze, his eyes narrowed and a sly smile pulled at his lips. "How's the boss?"

Bastard.

All eyes were on Fabian. Another friend from Harvard grad school, Konrad Korr, cut in before Fabian could respond. "Working with your dad now?" His accent thicker than usual. Konrad was the workaholic of the group. Even though he was a couple years older, he'd already run three businesses since graduating from the MBA program three years prior. Not that it was a surprise, Konrad's father was a successful businessman in

Germany. That's where he learned to be a workaholic.

"Nope." Ty's smile grew wider. Fabian shook his head, knowing Ty intended to rat him out. So much for keeping his secret. "He's working for Toni Robuchon." There it was, hanging in the dense air for their friends to pause, making sure they heard right.

Fabian remained calm, though punching Ty in the face seemed like a good idea. They were good at ragging on each other without mercy, had been since they were kids. Even after Dallas turned to Ty with a questioning gaze, Fabian remained tight-lipped.

"Toni Robuchon," Ty repeated, glancing at Dallas whose dark eyes grew rounder as realization set in.

"As in Antonia Robuchon? Private school Toni Robuchon? As in Bradley's ex-fiancée?" Apparently everyone knew about Toni and Stephan.

"That's the one." Fabian refused to react. If they had any indication he liked Toni, he wouldn't hear the end of it. Ty wouldn't hear the end of it later when he could get him alone.

Dallas, who'd been sitting on the sideline, was thoroughly flabbergasted. "Why is Toni your boss? How did that happen?"

"Who's Toni Robuchon?" Konrad asked in between his own sip of expensive scotch. He was the only one to have good taste in liquor, according to Fabian. He also didn't know any of the people they'd been talking about since he'd just moved to Houston that spring.

Fabian ignored Ty and Dallas, turning his attention to Konrad. "She's someone we went to school with. Her family owns Robuchon Investments."

"Ah, I'm familiar with the name." Konrad nodded. "Good firm."

"The old man wants me to get my feet wet in the

business world before he makes me partner at PE."
Fabian still hadn't looked at Ty or Dallas.

"Why is Toni your boss, though? Did her mother make her manager of something?" Dallas asked, leaning forward when the music began to thump louder. A crowd started to form. Fabian would rather be checking out the girls than talking anymore about Toni. Well, not really. He'd just rather not talk about Toni with the guys. The less he talked, the less they'd really know what was going on in his head in regards to her.

Ty cut in. "Nope. CEO." Could he not keep his damn mouth shut?

Fabian glared at him, shaking his head. Toni was the last secret he'd ever tell Ty.

Dallas's eyes grew wide. "CEO? No shit!"

"You're asking the wrong question, Halman." Ty at times referred to Dallas by his last name. He took a sip of his sissy drink and chewed on the straw in a slow churn.

Fabian threw up his hands in the air, finally showing the disdain he forced down inside. "And what's that question, Ty?" As Fabian asked the question, he caught a glimpse of a white dress in the distance. Small and fitted, the garment was made for the body wearing it. He dragged his gaze up the sky-high heels to the delicate ankles and calves. Up and over the knees to linger over the familiar curved backside. He knew her. When he caught sight of the woman in the white dress, he wasn't surprised it was Toni. Beautiful was the only way to describe her. Stunning would work too. And he wanted her.

"You can't dip your pen in the company ink, dude," Ty said, laughing.

"Fuck off, man." Fabian chuckled for show, his eyes still on Toni. "Have some more sissy punch."

"You trying to hit that?" Dallas joined in the laughter, his words pulling Fabian's attention.

"Really, man? Have some respect." Fabian didn't laugh anymore. In fact, he was pissed at the crude question. "No, I'm not trying to hit that." Yes, he certainly did want to hit that. So did the many men standing near her at the bar, trying to get her attention.

"Easy man, I'm just kidding." Dallas threw his hands up.

Fabian stood with the intention to greet her. "She's not my type."

"Bullshit," Ty said, pointing to the bar. "Speak of the devil."

"More like you're not hers." Dallas looked at her as well, admiration in his eyes. Calling dibs on her was becoming a powerful force.

"Nice-looking bird," Konrad commented with his British vernacular. "Might I suggest you talk her up before some other bloke does."

"I'm not going to talk her up," Fabian said, though that was exactly what he was going to do. "Just saying hi."

The guys laughed in unison. "*Right!*" Ty said, Dallas joining in with his own commentary.

The guys shouted after him as he stepped out of the VIP nook. Outside the space was louder if that was possible, throbbing with energy from the mixed crowd of both young professionals just out of college and society brats looking for another way to spend their father's money.

He slid his right hand through the top of his hair, the other hand still clutched his nearly empty glass. Not even thirty seconds later, he was in front of her, checking out the white dress that captured his attention. Close up she was even more gorgeous.

"Nice dress." The words were deliberately paced, but may have come off awkward and not cool as he intended.

She turned, her dark eyes pinning his. Her eyebrow lifted. "That's inappropriate, Mr. Pallis."

Despite her words, the pulse at her throat quickened. He was standing close enough to smell her sweet scent.

"Why?" He leaned in further, his lips too close to her ear. "It's after work hours."

She pulled back, a short breath slipped through her lips. "I know it is."

Their gazes connected again, and everything disappeared. She was the only thing he saw. In that crowded bar, he only saw her. "Say thank you then."

Her gaze narrowed. "Thank you then."

And just like that, she turned away and he became aware of everyone else again.

The woman peering over Toni caught his attention. Taller and attractive, though not like Toni, he racked his brain to identify her. He knew her from somewhere... *Oh, shit.* A conquest? Toni looked amused at him. She wouldn't be if she thought the other woman was a past hookup. In fact, Toni would never change her opinion of him if she thought that. God, he hoped the woman wasn't.

"Hi," her friend said, thrusting her hand in front of Toni against the bar to shake his. "I'm Melina, Toni's best friend. Nice to meet you."

"Best friend, you say?" He grinned, taking her soft hand into his. *Thank God.* He didn't know her.

Toni broke apart their connected hands with the intention to pass through. "I'm going to the ladies' room. If he doesn't leave you alone, call security."

"I honestly am not sure if she's kidding or not."

He watched the pull of her dress with each step she took. *Such a perfect ass*. He shook his head. It was unfair walking around like she did, commanding everyone as she did. He thought of the meeting earlier and what she'd said. This woman had no idea how powerful she was. She could have everything she wanted, if she just believed in herself.

"You like her." Melina yanked him from his thoughts.

"What?" He turned to her shining brown eyes.

"You just watched her walk away with that far-off look in your eyes. I saw it!" She gaped, as the bartender placed a Cosmo in front of her.

"Charge the ladies' drinks to Pallis."

"Thank you!" Melina smiled, lifting the glass to her lips. If she had enough Cosmos, she might forget what she saw. But with his luck lately, Fabian doubted it would be that easy.

"You have crush on your boss." She sat the drink on the wooden bar top. "What about Camille? Aren't you with her?"

His stomach jerked. That was how he knew her. "I thought you looked familiar. How do you know Camille?"

"I don't really. I know her from Pilates class. But we aren't friends. You probably saw me there. I've seen you pick her up before." She leaned on her elbow against the bar.

He shook his head with more intensity than he'd like. "No, we aren't together. I see other people. Well, I was. Not anymore."

"Not anymore?" Melina cocked her head. She didn't believe him.

He glanced to the ladies' room, desperately waiting for the white dress to emerge. "Not anymore." He turned back to her narrowed gaze.

She hesitated for a few beats. "You know, I sort of think Toni likes you. Sort of. But don't tell her I said that. She's very guarded right now because of her ex-fiancé." Her eyebrows lifted.

She sort of likes me? Not what he expected to hear. Actually, he thought she hated him with every fiber of his being. But this … this was the best news he could expect. What was better than that nugget of information? The thought energized him. "She's very guarded." He glanced to the restrooms again. Toni was nowhere in sight, and he was feeling bold. Where the hell was she?

"Go to the VIP section. My friends are hanging out there." He left Melina at the bar with the idea that she 'sort of likes him' fueling his next move.

* * * *

Of all the bars Toni could have gone to, why did she choose the one he chose? There were thousands of bars in Houston. What were the odds? His presence took her off kilter. Completely ruined her Zen, again. Okay not Zen, but he did ruin her girl's night out. She closed her eyes, recalled the moment he came up to her at the bar. The jerk. Who also happened to look amazing in his jeans. Men should look like that in jeans. *Ugh. Stop thinking about his perfect ass in those jeans*. She realized what he was doing there. Babe hunting.

Toni slipped a fifty-dollar bill into the bathroom attendant's jar, promptly turning away. On the other side of the door was the short dark hall feeding into the dance floor. She stepped into the darkness, legs shaking under her. She was about to give Fabian a piece of her mind, and save Mel from his moves.

"Come dance with me, love."

The familiar hand grabbed her arm, leading her to the dance floor. She couldn't find the strength to pull away after she confirmed who it was.

Stephan.

She was completely taken off guard. Again. The two men she didn't want to see couldn't leave her alone. In seconds, Stephan was gripping her hips as he moved erratically. Normally, he was a decent dancer. What he was doing now was embarrassing and clearly the result of too much alcohol. He leaned over—reeking of gin—and pressed his lips to her ear. Her skin crawled.

"I missed you, Antonia."

His hands rode up her rib cage. The horrible dream didn't stop there.

"I want you. I want to try again. Do you?"

How could he think this was acceptable?

She attempted to say one single word—*No!*—but nothing came out of her mouth. Any verbal skill had left her, and she could only focus on keeping the vodka and champagne down. The situation was dire at best. Toni stared at him, all the memories coming back to her at once. Loving him. Hating him. Wishing he was dead. Wanting him again. Hating him even more. Kicking him out of her office.

He spoke instead when she didn't. "Just dance with me."

She pushed away, though he caught her hand before she could free herself. "I don't want to."

"Come on, love." His face creased with his sloppy plea. "You don't mean it. I know you. You want to be with me."

Six months ago, she might have said yes. Hell, two months ago she might have. Not this month. And not ever again.

She shook her head, pulling hard with a surge of energy that ran through her. "Let me go." Blue eyes iced over—the man didn't like rejection. His grasp tightened.

"You don't mean that." A few dancers turned their way as she yanked again, causing a scene.

"Let me go, Stephan!" Just as she yanked again, someone came up behind her. A large hand reached over her, gripping Stephan's shoulder.

"You want to let her go?" *Oh God*. She knew that voice.

Fabian. Relief flooded her as Stephan dropped his hand.

Stephan pressed his lips together, nostrils flaring. He pulled back from Fabian's hold. Red-faced and furious with the intrusion, Stephan growled, "This isn't your business, Pallis."

Though she couldn't see Fabian, his body warmed her. When she turned, she faced Fabian's broad chest and fell into him. Against him, she found the strength she needed to fight Stephan.

"Get away from my girl," Stephan snarled, pulling her back to him, though she resisted. He'd been too strong for her. Fabian, on the other hand, remained calm, despite the vein throbbing at his neck.

Her gaze met Fabian's. He'd done it again. He came to her rescue.

Chapter Ten

Fabian could kill Stephan. No woman deserved to be treated the way he treated Toni. Fabian would never hurt a woman physically. He watched Toni shift in her dress, as she got herself together. Was she okay? Had she been hurt? If she was, Stephan had another problem on his hands. "Toni, come and have a drink with me and my friends."

"She doesn't associate with the help," Stephan snapped, pulling her close again. Couldn't he keep his hands off her? If she was any closer to him, she'd be inside his shirt.

"Yes, thank you. I will have a drink with you." She surprised them both.

"What?" Stephan's disbelief brought a smile to Fabian's face. "You can't be serious."

She broke free from Stephan. "Oh, I'm very serious." The strength Fabian knew she had finally showed. "I already told you I don't want you. Nothing you can do or say will change my mind. Got it?" She didn't wait for his response. Stephan wouldn't have a response for a while by the look on his face. She grabbed Fabian's sleeve. "Let's go."

Fabian shrugged, no words needed. They left Stephan paralyzed on the dance floor, still assessing what had just happened. Fabian himself hardly believed it. He followed her, but not to the VIP nook where his friends were. Releasing his arm as they approached the bar, she looked at him. Her eyes welled up.

So many thoughts ran through his head. He didn't know what to feel. What did it mean?

"Thank you for that." Her gaze dropped for a moment, but lifted once more to meet his eyes.

Again it was just her in the bar, and him. Everyone else went away. "I didn't like the way he treated you." He stepped closer to her, close enough to hear her breath. "I would never treat a woman that way. Especially not you. You didn't deserve that." There, he said it.

"How do you know what I deserve?" She was completely breathless.

"I know you deserve better than that dick." She looked away. With a finger under her chin, he lifted up her face. "I mean it."

Gulping, she wrapped her fingers around his wrist. "I should go."

Toni didn't move a muscle though, and neither did he. Seconds passed, yet they stayed that way. His finger under her chin, her fingers wrapped around his wrist. Each taking in the other and the predicament they found themselves in. Her lips tempted him. He zeroed in on them. God, he wanted to kiss her. It was the perfect opportunity. She'd dropped her stonewalls for him and putting on his playboy act was the furthest thing from his mind.

"I really want to ki—"

"Will you dance with me?" Her eyes were wide, thundering with emotions. Mel had been right. He could feel it in his bones. But Toni didn't sort of like him, she *liked* him. No denying it.

Fabian's heart pounded in his ears. "Of course, I'll dance with you."

Nothing could take Fabian off his high. Not the prospect of Stephan waiting in the wings, ready to strike. Not the notion of his friends carrying on like maniacs at the sight of him so close to Toni on the dance floor. Nothing. Toni wanted to be close to him. Touching him. Moving with him to the music. He hoped this wouldn't be the last time she felt that way. He would do anything he could to maintain their connection. The need for her attention—any crumb of attention—was strong enough to make him feel unsure of himself. Insecure even. Vulnerable was the better word for it. That was a new feeling for him. He guessed women he'd dated might have felt that way about him—waiting for his crumbs. What a shitty feeling. Control-less feeling. Yet, there he was waiting for more attention from her.

He spun her just as they stepped on the dance floor. He pulled her close by her shoulders, careful not to touch the parts he really wanted to. A wrong move and he could be kicked to the curb. No way in hell would he end up like Stephan. Her body waved to the beat, hips moving against him. While he'd been known for some smooth moves, he had nothing on her. He kept up with her nonetheless.

Her smile grabbed him. Snatched him completely. His body pulsed with the throbbing music. When she pulled him close, he wasn't sure he could keep his hands only on her shoulders anymore. Her lips moved against his ear. "You're a good dancer."

"Just following your lead."

"Shouldn't I be following your lead?"

They locked gazes. All movement stopped. Her smile faded, but her eyes sparkled. The anger toward Stephan resurfaced. He needed her to know how good she was. "You're way too good for Stephan. Did you know that? *Do* you know that?"

Everything they just had slipped away. It was too much for her. For him, it wasn't nearly enough. She looked away from him, the coldness he'd felt before returned. Antonia Robuchon, acting CEO had emerged. No, he couldn't accept it after how she just danced with him. After the way she looked at him.

Her weak attempt to pull away failed. She didn't really try to free herself of him, which solidified his belief that she did like him. And he was about to let her know how much he liked her too. He pulled her in close, his lips touching the shell of her ear. "If you were mine, I would never let you go."

"I—"

Fabian put a finger over her lips, her eyes closed in response. Every part of him needed to kiss her. He wanted to feel her lips on his more than he wanted to take his next breath. The notion winded him. More than that, the need to protect and care for her was foreign and disconcerting. He literally would have done anything to protect her from Stephan. Just then, a tug on his arm took him from the space where only he and Toni existed.

He turned, annoyed. "What?" The person didn't register at first. The silhouette outlined a perfect figure, tall and curving. Any other day he would have known exactly who it belonged to. Yet still, the only thing he knew was the abandonment on his hip when Toni's hand fell with the interruption.

The woman came into view under the dance floor lights. They shined on her face, catching her narrowed blue eyes and firm pressed lips. Camille stood before him. *Ah, shit.*

Camille didn't bother to look at Toni. "Who is this, Fabian?"

"I'm his boss," Toni said, commanding both their attention. "And he's all yours." She pivoted on her heels, walking across the dance floor to the entrance before Fabian could have a second thought.

Camille wrapped her arms around his waist, pulling him to her. "She's right about one thing. You *are* all mine. Don't forget it."

He jerked away from her, putting an arm's length

distance between them. "No, Cam, I'm not yours. I've told you that so many times." Fabian glanced to his friends in the VIP nook who didn't seem the wiser, which he was grateful for. Melina had their undivided attention though. He turned to Camille, dreading whatever else she had to say, but could only focus on his need to go after Toni.

Camille crossed her arms over her banded crop top. She was a gorgeous woman, no doubt. But he acknowledged something then that he hadn't for many years. He needed more than a gorgeous body. It wasn't enough for him to chase physical beauty anymore. Not since Toni. Camille studied him, realization setting in. "You can't tell me you like your boss, Fabian. Are you serious?"

Scrubbing his face, he let out the longest sigh of his life. What he had to tell her—again—would be painful—once more. He chose his words carefully, and with as much sensitivity as he could in the middle of a dance floor. "Cam, you're a nice girl, but I can't give you what you want. I never could. I told you many times. So this should not be a surprise." That was the best way he could say it. Again. Big globes of tears formed at the corner of each eye. *Not the tears.* He looked away. Why did she always have to cry? Couldn't she see that he sucked as a potential boyfriend? Not that he actually ever was a potential boyfriend. She stepped closer, hooking a finger in between the space between buttons on his shirt. He removed her hand. "I can't do this with you every time, Cam. I have to go. I'm sorry." He turned from her, eyes straining to see the entrance. He needed to find Toni.

He glanced back to Camille who struggled with another breakdown. He was so sorry. Not just for the way he treated women, but for the way he knew they wanted him, waited for him. But he didn't feel anything for any of them. Not like what he felt for Toni out on the dance floor, or then as he was desperate to find her. The urge to chase Toni made him feel even sorrier for what he'd done. Before he could rationalize everything he felt, he raced to the front near the opening of the dark hall connecting the lounge to the main entrance.

Destiny was on his side. Toni slumped against the wall, totally vulnerable, with her eyes closed. At first, Fabian thought she'd been crying, but as he grew closer, he saw her fists tightly bound at her sides. She was upset.

He found his voice once he was only a foot from her. "You're not just my boss, Toni."

Her eyelids shot open. Her lips parted, mirroring his own.

Something took over him. Something stronger than his will, and before he knew what happened, he palmed her face, lifting her chin until her mouth met his in a crushing kiss. The ground fell from under his feet with that kiss. He was totally disoriented until his tongue touched hers and he found his stability. They tangled together, fused like one mass moving in harmony to the throbbing bass pounding against the wall. The kiss was wet and savage and made him so hard he wasn't sure he could separate from her.

She wanted it. He knew she did. As much as he wanted it. Everything built up to that moment. She kneaded his arms, and then dragged her fingers up his rib cage. He groaned, kissing her harder, sucking on her lips, biting her, tasting her. She returned his intensity. But when his hands fell to her throat and down her décolletage, she turned her face, breaking away from him.

"We can't."

* * * *

Her lips throbbed with his kiss, left her feeling

raw and abandoned. He was a good kisser. Probably good at other things too. She couldn't let her mind go there. Too much could go wrong. A broken heart would be the first of many things if she let this go any further.

"You have a girlfriend, or friends. I don't know what you call them." She pushed him away, ignoring the dazed look in his eyes and the stumble in his step. Touching the swollen skin around her mouth, she could still feel the tingling burn from his scruff.

As Fabian wiped his mouth, she turned away with the intention of putting as many footsteps between them as possible, but he spun her around by the shoulder. Something desperate in his eyes pulled at her heartstrings. "I don't have girlfriends. I don't have anyone."

She actually believed him.

But he was good at getting his way. Yesterday, she would've had no problem second-guessing herself about him. In fact that morning, she'd dismissed anything he said about not having girlfriends. The proof was all over the Internet. The proof faced her minutes ago on the dance floor.

But the way his bright green eyes pleaded with her … it was so strange to see. She wasn't sure how to proceed—if she should proceed.

"It doesn't matter, Fabian. What happened out there, whatever it was, should not have happened. It's completely inappropriate. I'm sorry." She fought all her urges to take back what she'd said. He looked so gorgeous and tormented. Of all the things that made her want him, it was how vulnerable he looked. This Fabian blew the Fabian she'd known out of the water. The more she thought about what was happening between them, the more torn she became. Mr. Pallis, his own father, said Fabian had a way with women. Was this what he meant?

Because she was willing to give Fabian the benefit of believing him. Believing that the man in front of her was real.

I need to get out of here.

"Antonia!" he called to her as she walked away without another word. "Please don't go."

Against her better judgment, she stopped and turned to face those mesmerizing eyes again. How could things be normal on Monday? "No, Fabian. This was a mistake."

His lips parted, still plump from their kiss. The pulse at his throat beat through his skin. She counted them. *One. Two. Three. Four.* Silence ruled, despite the DJ music still blaring through the building. She'd blocked it out. Everything was blocked out. When she didn't think she could hold her breath any longer, he spoke caution he'd never employed in all their other conversations.

"You can't tell me there is nothing between us."

How easily she could lose herself with that statement. Despite everything, it was true. She kissed him back because she wanted it just as desperately. But the moment had passed, and she had to reject him for the business's sake. More importantly, for her heart's sake. Even if she thought she could be wrong about him, she couldn't take that chance. Not again.

She leveled her gaze at him, forcing herself to stay composed.

"There's nothing between us, Mr. Pallis."

He winced at her harsh words, but it didn't stop her from walking away from him. He didn't follow her either. Not that she expected him to after the expression on his face. Once she'd emerged out into the humid air on Congress Street, she gasped. Leaving him that way was much harder than she thought it would be.

Toni pulled out her cell phone from her clutch bag. Miles came around the driver side of the limo, swift to open the back door for her. She ignored the concern on his face. Stepping in, she slammed the door despite Miles holding on the handle. She pulled out her phone to text Melina.

Toni: **Mel, I have to leave. Don't worry, Miles will take you home or anywhere else you want to go.**

Mel: **Wtf happened? I saw Stephan? Did he confront you? I'm in the VIP section w/ F's friends. Where is he? They keep asking me…**

Toni: **Everything is fine. Yes, Steph showed up. Camille showed up too. No problems, I just don't feel well. Please stay and have fun.**

Mel: **Are you sure? I don't want you to go home :/ F's friends are hilarious lol**

Toni: **Positive! I'll call you tomorrow.**

Mel: **K. Brunch tomorrow?**

Toni: **For sure!**

Soon enough she was safe in her penthouse. Toni mulled over what happened against her better judgment. While in the shower over-soaping her body, she imagined Fabian's fingers on her when they danced. Later in her bed when she'd calmed, she could only think about one thing. The kiss. His lips on hers, warm and wet. He might have been the best kisser she'd ever had. Closing her eyes, she lifted her fingers to her lips, still feeling the sensations. Her whole body sizzled thinking about how he's touched her. For at least an hour—maybe more—she was obsessed with trying to remember each moment with him. Deep inside, she throbbed. Ripples of desire waved through her body. Slow at first, then faster until the end point was at the apex of her thighs. Wanton need drove her to continue.

Slipping her hand into her cotton panties, she

moved down until she found the source of her ache. She envisioned Fabian touching her in that spot. She wanted Fabian to touch her. To be inside her. With those thoughts, she found her own fingers bringing herself to pleasure. "Fabian," she moaned, moving faster against herself until the sensations burst inside her and she called out his name again.

Afterward, she wiped her brow, feeling perplexed and disoriented at the same time. Toni couldn't find her bearings. The air conditioning turned on, blowing a stream of cold air on her. She turned over to hide her face in the pillow in shame. *I'm screwed.*

Chapter Eleven

At exactly eight-fifteen on Monday morning, Fabian placed a cup of coffee on Toni's desk. Exactly how she required. She faced her computer screen, completely unaware of him until the porcelain cup hit the desk. She turned, surprised. Both glorious dark eyes turned up to him. The sun emerged from under a cloud just as she faced him. Clearly, God was jacking with him. As cliché as it sounded, she looked like an angel. All she needed was a halo and a pair of wings. Victoria's Secret wings maybe. He digressed.

"Fabian." His name fell from her nude lips in a breathy voice. Her gaze dropped to the cup, and then back to him again.

"Three-fourths cup French roast coffee, one-fourth cup organic skim milk, and three packets of cane sugar." He imagined Friday night again. Dancing with her. Kissing her. He couldn't forget it. Would she bring it up? "Just how you like it."

She nodded. "Thank you."

That's it? That's all I get? The words gutted him. Surely she had more to say than thank you. "You're welcome."

She turned back to her computer screen. He waited, counting to ten. Nothing. Though he knew he should leave—clearly she was done with him—he simply couldn't let it go. Friday needed to be discussed, despite what she might think. "We should talk about what happened Friday."

"I don't know what you mean." The clicking of her keyboard followed.

Did she really think she could avoid the conversation? How insulting. And frankly, he was pissed.

Heat emanated from his body, making him feel like he wore a radiator instead of a suit. "Toni, don't play with me."

"I'm not." Keyboard still clicking, he wanted to yank the damn thing from under her fingers.

He raked a hand through his hair, tension rising up his spine. "We kissed."

No more keyboard clicks, only silence. He heard her deliberate sigh. "Yes."

"And you liked it." His anger was getting the best of him, and he wanted to be rational when he discussed their kiss. Especially since his feelings for her had only grown stronger. Even in the face of her nonchalance, he still felt connected to her. Calmer, he challenged her. "You wanted it, Toni, as much as I did. Can you admit it at least?"

Of all the things she could have said or done—admit it, deny it, throw him out of her goddamn office—she remained still, eyes downcast on her keyboard. It wasn't like her to be subdued, especially when he spoke to her the way he did, without a filter. "I won't do that."

"Why?" Moving close, he acted on pure impulse and curved his hand over her narrow shoulder. He needed to touch her. "Why won't you?" he asked again, that time with more force out of sheer frustration.

She stood, the chair rolling from under her with the act. "Because I'll want to do it again and I know we can't do that again. Okay? Are you happy now?"

He grabbed her, practically lifting her off her toes as he pulled her close to him. "No, I'm not happy. I won't be happy until you admit to yourself that you want me as much as I want you." The space between them grew short and tense. Energy spun around them, making his heart nearly burst inside him. But he didn't care, his lips were so close to her, he would die if he didn't kiss her.

She yelped, closing her eyes. "Fabian!" A desperate cry escaped her

"I'm going to kiss you, Toni, and I don't think you can stop me."

Just before his lips crashed on hers, she whispered, "I won't try to."

Nothing mattered in those hot, fully-charged seconds. He devoured her like it was the last thing he'd do. Not even the fact that the door wasn't locked stopped him. Anyone could walk in and he didn't give a shit. Maybe he wanted someone to walk in. Wanted someone else to witness what he feared might be just a figment of his imagination.

Her mouth opened with the same hunger he felt inside. Tasting her tongue was like tasting heaven. Sweet. Otherworldly. She intoxicated him with every nip of his mouth. Every suck. Nothing could be enough for him after that. He needed more.

He lifted her off her flat shoes, putting her on the desk, not caring papers and other items fell off in a small crash to the floor. Her cotton skirt rode up her thighs where she sat, but she didn't stop clinging to him.

"I want you so much, Toni."

He parted her legs with both hands gliding up her smooth skin until her red panties emerged. She gasped as he cupped her sex fully, and when she bit her bottom lip, eyes at half-mast, his mouth watered with anticipation. Leaning back on her hands, she turned her face, eyes still closed. His kissed her throat. Licked her delicate skin. Bit it. As he trailed hot, wet kisses down her chest, he unbuttoned her plain white blouse, exposing a matching red lace bra. Instantly, his fingers circled around her back, curling over her ribcage. Smooth skin made him groan.

"God, you're so beautiful." He sucked her

cleavage, leaving marks behind. Perfect was the only way to describe her.

He lifted her bra over both perky breasts, catching one dusty pink nipple in his mouth. She whimpered, eliciting a moan from him. Her moans turned him on so much that he knew her pleasure was more important. Relieving her desire was his mission.

He slid his fingers over her hips to her exposed lace panties.

"Fabian," she gasped when he pulled the scrap of material off without warning, revealing her dark pink flesh, plump and ready for him.

"Yes," he said, swiping a finger over her hardened clitoris. She moaned, urging him on. Again he rubbed her, wetting his finger with her arousal. It was a herculean effort to contain his own arousal when he wanted to be inside her. But this wasn't about him.

He slipped a finger in her, feeling her body grab him as he delved further inside. "That's so good." His voice was husky. "You're so tight. So tight." She cried out. The both of them had obviously forgotten where they were. Not that he gave a rat's ass. "I bet you taste like heaven."

"Fabian, please," she begged.

Holy shit. The realization hit him like a ton of brick. He had her. She succumbed to her feelings for him finally. If he screwed up, he'd never forgive himself. He ran his fingers over her most private part, making her moan. Sliding deep again, he drove his finger inside her. She clenched around him, telling she was close to climax.

"Oh, God, Fabian. Oh, God." She rolled back her head as he continued with his feat. His excitement grew tenfold. He wouldn't stop until he heard the sweet sound of her orgasm.

Buzz!

The sound shocked him. It might as well have been a bomb siren.

"Miss Robuchon, there is a Camille Carano to see Fabian. Is he in your office?" The voice on the intercom forced them back to reality. And it was a harsh reality.

The fog of what they'd just done weighed heavily on his ability to find a coherent thought. Stunned, still, he blinked, trying to orient himself. Flashes of seconds past, him, Toni, her office, hands in her panties. It seemed unreal, but his deflating erection proved otherwise. It was very real.

"Oh, my God!" Toni jumped up from the desk, reassembling her clothes with fervor.

"Miss Robuchon?" The voice on the other end of the line was sounded perplexed.

"Umm … uh…Yes, he is. Tell her to wait about five minutes, please." She punched the intercom button.

Fabian was desperate for Toni to say something to him. Something that could reconnect them. She felt so far away. "Toni." Her name was hoarse on his tongue. He stepped closer. "Antonia."

With a sharp turn, she faced him. "No." Stormy eyes met his. Scrubbing her face with firm hands, she groaned. "I should be fired for this."

"We like each other, Toni. There is nothing wrong here."

She chuckled lightly like it was a joke or a damn shame. Maybe both. He braced himself for what she would say next. "You aren't good for me. I can't like a player." She buttoned the last button, taking a good look at him before she said, "I won't."

His heart sank in his chest.

* * * *

How could she let it get that far? No matter what she wanted, Fabian was not right for her. She would end up with a broken heart and showing up at his place of employment just like the others. No, she wouldn't be like all the others.

Toni straightened. "Your Camille is waiting for you."

"She's not my Camille." His eyes were so green, she had to stare a second longer at the beauty of them. When he reached out to her, she thought she might change her mind.

"It doesn't matter to me." Who was she trying to convince?

"You're so full of it, Toni. You were just kissing me like I was going to war, and had that stupid intercom not gone off, you would have come so hard with just my finger." His crude words excited her. *Turn away.* Her resolve would have to be stronger than his.

"You don't really want me, Fabian. You want to conquer me like you do all your other women. All the time. If you had me, you'd probably lose interest. I don't really want to be another Camille in the lobby waiting to see you. That's not my style."

The edges of his mouth fell. "Wow. That's harsh. Not really sure I deserved that from you."

"It's called planning ahead." The look on his face stabbed her heart. The power was hers, and she used it for him and in spite of him, convincing herself it was for the best.

Silence. He had nothing to say it would seem, which was best. What else was there to say? She'd made her peace. Of course he had to have the last word. But he was different. When he looked at her with those eyes, she was transported back to H Bar. To the Fabian who rescued her, who she danced with. "You're wrong about me."

The intercom buzzed again. Damn intercom.

"Miss Robuchon, may I send her back?"

"Yes." The silence echoed in her office. After all the things she said to him, she still managed to hate the fact that Camille was waiting for him in the lobby. "Your Camille is on the way."

"She's not my Camille," he insisted again.

She scoffed in response. That was the way she knew how to deal with her feelings for him. Inside, she knew she was wrong. But she'd made her decision. When the knock at the door diluted the tension between them, she walked over to open it.

On the other side of the frosted glass door, Camille stood like some gorgeous Amazon with long legs coming out of tiny black shorts, feet adorned with strappy heeled sandals. Her dark hair was pulled to the side over one shoulder, and her face perfectly made up. No one could argue she was striking. She was damn near perfect, and Toni felt a tinge of jealousy to think Fabian had shared the perfect Camille's bed numerous times.

She wearily smiled up at Camille who was probably a foot taller than her, especially since Toni wore flats. "He's all yours." She said it again ironically.

Camille's narrowed gaze scanned the office until they locked on Fabian. "Hi, Fabes."

"You should have called first, Camille," Fabian said with a stern tone. Toni figured he talked to them all like that, especially when they just showed up unannounced.

"Fabian, take your guest into your office and don't interrupt me for the rest of the day. Understand?" Toni placed a hand on her hip, emphasizing the point with a raised eyebrow.

He nodded, staring at her longer than he needed to before he strode to his office with Camille on his heels. Once the door shut, Toni released a sigh the size of

Canada.

This is a disaster.

She retrieved her chair, sitting heavily in it. Her mother would kill her if she knew what she had done with Fabian—the assistant. Nothing about their relationship was professional anymore, and she would have to figure out how to restore the power balance between them. If it was possible.

While deep in thought, the phone rang a dozen times. Maybe more. Her first inclination was to let the call rollover to voicemail, but as she glanced at the caller ID, she jumped to answer the call. "Mom, are you okay?" Her heart pounded.

"Hi Antonia, dear. I got the most wonderful visit this morning." Surprised by her jovial voice, Toni smiled. Her mother hadn't been that happy in months.

"From who?" Toni furrowed her brow.

"Stephan! He came by to say hello."

"What?" Her voice dropped an octave, her heart dropped too. "What do you mean he came by?"

"Don't be silly, Antonia. You know very well what he came by means."

Toni closed her eyes. Not him. The Friday incident came to mind. If only her mother knew what Stephan did to her, she might not be so joyous. "What did he want? Besides to say hello."

"He just wanted to see how I am—"

She opened her eyes, focusing on the caller ID. "And did you tell him?"

"I did tell him I had been ill. I mean he could clearly see that I am not well."

Antonia shifted her gaze to the ceiling. "You didn't want anyone to know, Mom. Why would you tell Stephan?"

"He was practically my son-in-law, Antonia. I

knew him for many years until you…" She stopped.

"Until he left me for another girl?" Toni barked, not entirely surprised her mother seemed to take his side. She'd always liked Stephan, wanted him to be part of the family. A lump formed in her throat. She couldn't forget her mother was ill and couldn't take an argument. "I'm sorry, Mom. I didn't mean to sound that way."

"We all make mistakes, dear. All of us." Toni always hated their unbearable silences. Judgments passed in those silences. "He expressed wanting to reunite with you and our family."

"He *what*?" Toni's mouth fell open. *How dare he bring my mother into this!*

"I think it would be a smart idea to let him redeem himself. The Bradleys really are the best suited to be a part of the Robuchon empire. It's been a sort of understanding between the families. You know that. I don't see a prospect for you right now. Especially if that useless Pallis kid is the only male contact you've had. I wish you would get out more."

"Fabian isn't useless. He did very well at Harvard." She couldn't believe she actually said the words.

"Dear God, don't tell me you like that boy." Her mother spit, not hiding her disgust.

"No!" Toni said quickly. Calmer, and more contained, she added. "I think he's a loose cannon and a chauvinist." She dropped her face in her palm. No way could she describe how she really felt about him to her mother.

"I've arranged a dinner with you and Stephan tomorrow night at L'Atelier for eight. I told him it would be the three of us, but you will have to make an excuse for me. I'm not feeling well at the moment. And I doubt I'll get better by tomorrow."

"Of course you're not, Mom. You're in the middle of chemotherapy." The words choked her. Having dinner with Stephan would choke her as well. But how could she deny her mother? She hadn't been that happy since before the cancer diagnosis. At least not how Helene Robuchon defined happy.

"Thank you for reminding me, Antonia." Her sarcasm shined through, just like the mother Toni had always known.

How could she tell her mother she didn't want anything to do with Stephan? "Mom, I'm not sure about dinner with Stephan. I was really hurt. Don't you remember?"

"You two were very young. Maybe he got cold feet. That isn't unusual. But, after talking with him, I do believe he is ready to make a real commitment. He wants to make it with you. I think it would be foolish not to give him a chance. Both families are in agreement."

She sighed, eye closed tight. "So the families talked about this?" *Behind my back?* And when the hell did the families have a chance to talk about it? It had only been a few days since she saw Stephan again.

"Darling, you're doing this. It's what you wanted before. You'll see that now he is even more the man you could ever want."

More than anything she wanted to bring up Friday and what Stephan did. A zebra couldn't suddenly change its stripes just as Stephan couldn't suddenly be her knight in shining armor. That man probably didn't exist. She hated her life so much then, but she did what she knew was expected. "Fine. I'll have dinner with him."

Chapter Twelve

Tuesday morning, Fabian wore his lucky black and white polka dot bowtie. He really needed it. Everything was weird with Toni, and he didn't want it to be that way. Not with her. He'd stayed up all night mulling over what happened. In those moments on her desk, he knew she felt what he did. No denying it. Why was she determined to forget it? Act like it didn't happen at all.

In the office kitchen, he slipped a gallon of organic milk he'd bought that morning into the refrigerator. Davina didn't say much to him besides hello, which was fine with him. The only person on his mind was Toni. With the hope that Toni would soften toward him, he walked into Toni's office holding her special coffee. Empty. Where was she? He glanced at his watch. She should be at her desk. He put the coffee down on her RI coaster.

He waited for several minutes, and she'd still not arrived. Being late wasn't like her. Was she okay? Was she sick? He didn't want to think the worst. Worst would be she didn't want to see him. He should leave, or he'd spend the whole day waiting for her in that very spot. Reaching for a pen on her desk, he briefly thought about the note he intended to leave for her.

Miss Robuchon,

Meet me in conference room C to discuss new findings with NeuRx. I think you'll be pleased.

—F

The night before he'd managed to research the neurostimulation product Toni had been passionate about. He'd only done it to get her out of his mind. But what he found only made him think of her more. He couldn't wait to share the game changing information with her. The executives would beg Toni to lead RI once she presented the new information. Hopefully, Fabian would be in better standing with his father once he found out how capable his son was.

"What are you doing in here?" Toni startled him.

"Hey," he said, fingers still pressing the Post-it to her computer screen. "I wanted to meet with you."

She crossed her arms over her red blouse. Her lips matched perfectly. "About?"

"NeuRx," he said it slowly, trying to gauge her mood. He couldn't read her. "I've found some information you might be interested in."

Her arms dropped to her sides. "Oh?" Approaching her desk, she stopped a couple of feet in front of him.

"Yeah." He paused, his gaze sliding over her face. Dark circles rimmed her eyes. She looked tired. Restless. Had she not slept much the night before? Odd, she didn't seem interested in what he had to say about NeuRx. Something else occupied her thoughts, troubled her. Was it him that made her restless and tired? He needed to know what was going on with her. "I was surprised that you weren't here earlier."

"I-I had an appointment before work." She looked away.

He frowned, willing her to face him "Is everything okay?"

Sighing, she finally gazed up at him, her eyes empty. "Yes. Tell me about this new information."

"Here?" The office seemed too small somehow for the big news he had to share.

"Why not?"

He placed several sheets of paper on her desk he'd printed from home the night before. "I'll need to use your computer…"

She dragged her guest chair to him, letting him take it from her. Their fingers touched, sending a shock through him. His heart fluttered, and for a split second he thought how much he wanted to put her on the desk again. In seconds they'd sit side by side, elbows touching. When they were, he reveled in the warmth her body gave him.

The scent of vanilla wafted off her body. Every time her arm brushed up against his, the material of her blouse caressed him. He imagined it was her skin on his. His temperature rose steadily the longer they sat so close. Images of his fingers inside her the day before came at full speed, making his body tense in all the places he was trying to stay relaxed. He desperately wanted to know if she was thinking of it too.

Somehow thirty minutes passed with him losing his train of thought each time her blouse sleeve brushed against him. "So … so you see, our competitor, CapInvest, is already backing a clinical trial for a product with similar technology. Except, that surgery will be much more invasive. Though NeuRx can find another investment company, CapInvest's product will already be at FDA submission by that point and will most likely claim the US market by timing alone. We need to jump on this now."

She sat back, her blouse sleeve brushing against him again. "Wow. That's impressive research. How did you come across this?"

He shrugged. He liked the way her dark eyes shined at him in that moment. "I read an article on biomedical technology investments last night."

"You did all this research last night?" Her fingers touched his bicep.

He gazed down at her fingers, warm sensations

rushing through him. *Don't stop touching me.* "I didn't sleep a wink."

She'd become aware of her own hand on him. Snatching it away, she said, "Well it's brilliant. You're brilliant."

His heart stopped. No one had ever given him such a compliment. Not like that. Not with that look. "You saw an opportunity. Give yourself credit."

She shook her head, her voice softer than he'd ever heard it. "I don't know why your father doesn't make you partner."

How could he respond to that? She completely knocked him off kilter with her compliment. A one-eighty from the day before. Again, he replayed what happened between them, staring at her lips and hoping she didn't notice. A long pause stretched between them. Neither spoke. Maybe a whole minute passed before he said, "Let's just say a week ago I wasn't fit for partner."

"Now you are?" Dark eyes narrowed, lips curled slightly.

"Maybe I'm closer." She smiled at him, but it faded fast. He was compelled to tell her exactly what he felt about her. "I've never met anyone like you, Toni." She looked away immediately, the invisible walls coming up. He could see her disconnecting from him.

The distance between them grew. "Oh, I'm not that special."

"Then you don't see what I do."

She looked him square in the eyes, a bit annoyed and angry. "Oh really? What do you see?"

"I see someone who's misunderstood. Someone who wants to please, but maybe it comes at the cost of being vulnerable, which you have a hard time with." He wanted to go on because it was so easy to see these things. Things he saw in himself too.

"You don't know me at all." She turned, but he knew there was truth to what he said.

"So tell me something then," he challenged her.

"Like what?"

He shrugged. "Anything."

Facing him, she rolled her eyes. "This is so stupid."

"Why? You said I don't know you. Well, I want to know you. So tell me something."

She bit her bottom lip, chewing it. Fabian was quite amazed that she might actually tell him something real. They might have an actual conversation. After what seemed like an eternity, she said, "I want to be CEO. The real CEO." She stood, shaking from her revelation. "There, I told you something."

"Why can't you be CEO?" He stood too.

"Apparently, I don't have what it takes." She folded her arms over her chest.

"Bullshit. I don't buy that for a minute."

"*You* tell me something now." She changed the subject.

He laughed. "Like what?"

"Anything."

"Uh … okay." He raked his fingers through his hair. What could he say out loud that he'd never said to another person? In a moment of complete vulnerability, which was uncomfortable for him, he realized something about himself that he'd never faced. He looked at her as she waited patiently, and he knew in his heart his words would be safe with her. "I'm afraid to become like my father. But I'm just like him. When I have tons of women in my life, there is no one to leave me. But someone always leaves. I leave. I don't want to anymore."

God. The urge to walk away moved him. He'd been halfway to his office when she called to him.

"Fabian." She waited for him to turn. "I've never met anyone like you either."

* * * *

Fabian didn't say another word. His whole heart was on his sleeve for her alone, and it completely tore her apart. Fabian gets his way with women, but he *got* her with that. That admission changed what she thought of him. He wasn't what he seemed, and she was ashamed to have passed such harsh judgment on him. The playboy act was a front for his fear of being alone. And it made her sad for him.

Toni stood near the window, watching the cars and pedestrians on the street below. The view calmed her, soothed her mind. If not for the cell phone ringing in the background, she would have stayed there the rest of that day. Running to her bag under the desk, she grabbed the phone.

"Hi, Mel." She glanced at the clock. Eleven in the morning.

"Meet me for lunch?"

"Sure. Where?" She needed to get away. Once she'd written down the details, she hightailed it for the Robuchon limo.

They met at Melina's favorite sushi restaurant in Neartown. Toni was glad to get out of the office for a while, even if just for lunch. She needed to clear her head. Get away from Fabian and what they had revealed to each other. It was tragic and sad. She wondered if there was any hope for either of them. No hope for her, she mused, thinking on the dinner she would have with Stephan that night. Fabian had hope, she was sure of it. He was not what society painted him to be. He was much more.

"Toni, what's wrong?" Melina was reading her thoughts again.

Toni returned to reality, eyeing the glass of water—and waiter—in front of her. "Huh?"

Her friend narrowed her gaze and asked the waiter for a few more minutes. "Are you okay? You look like something's wrong."

Statement of the year. A lot was wrong that she didn't know how to begin to fix it. She cleared her throat, taking a sip of the ice cold water. Too cold. She shivered after. "Yeah … it's been a weird morning. But I'm okay." The feigned smile physically hurt her face.

"I was saying how I missed you on Saturday at brunch." Melina placed both elbows on the table.

"Oh, right." Toni had forgotten about that. An eternity of things had been stuffed into the span of four days. Saturday seemed like ages ago. "I just wasn't feeling well. Too much champagne I guess."

"You hardly had anything at the bar, though…"

Toni laid the cloth napkin over her thighs. She'd worn white slim pants that day, would be a shame to get dirty. "Low tolerance."

Melina's gaze narrowed again. "I guess…" She looked down to her menu, closing it not a few seconds later. "I know what I want."

"Me too," Toni said, though she hadn't looked at the menu.

Melina smiled and toyed with her own cloth napkin until the waiter came back to take their order. She fixed her gaze on Toni, who'd held her breath. "The guys and I thought you and Fabian left together on Friday."

"Well, we didn't!" Toni's body sizzled. Some patrons glanced their way. Attempting to regain her cool, Toni pushed a stray tendril behind her ear. "What *guys* are you talking about?" She knew what guys.

"Ty and those guys."

Toni sat back in her seat. "Oh…"

"I was with them when the whole … thing happened."

Toni averted her gaze. "What thing?" She knew damn well what thing. *Stop being an idiot.*

Melina's eyebrow lifted. "Really?"

Damn Melina. Toni shrugged. What else could she do? "Okay … fine. Yes, it was a bad situation. Stephan showed up again, drunk, and tried to win me back. Though, I use that phrase loosely." Stephan thought he had the right to take anything he wanted.

"What do you mean again?"

She sighed. Any other subject would be better than talk about Stephan. "He showed up at the office. He ran into Fabian at a restaurant and heard he was my assistant."

"Son of a bitch." Melina pressed her lips together. "He has a lot of nerve showing up after all the crap he put you through."

"He's insufferable." The heat spread over her face with her growing anger.

"So, let me get this straight. He doesn't want you, but he doesn't want anyone else to have you. Especially someone hot and rich like Fabian."

"There's no having going on here. Fabian just helped me out of a bind. That's all." Convincing Melina would be hard. Harder would be to convince herself.

"Okay," Melina started slowly. "But then you and Fabian were bumping and grinding on the dance floor. What was that about?"

Toni looked away, biting the insides of her cheek.

"Oh, my God. You really do like Fabian." Melina's voice rose an octave.

Toni met her gaze.

"That's crazy." She played with her wooden chopsticks. Several beats passed before she continued.

"And if I did …well, it just wouldn't work out anyway."

"He's not with Camille. I don't think he's with anyone right now."

Toni shook her head, remembering her conversation with him earlier, and knew the words she was about to say were wrong. "He's with everyone. I wouldn't want to be just another woman to him."

"But you want to be something?" Melina beamed.

"No, I don't want to be anything." Wrong again. Luckily, the waiter brought their seaweed salads. Toni stuffed her mouth to keep quiet. Conversation finally over.

Chapter Thirteen

Toni didn't talk to Fabian the rest of the day. In fact, she'd closed and locked her office door. Honestly, he didn't mind. His own door would have been closed too, but she never entered his office anyway. Over and over, he replayed their revelations to each other. Where the admission came from, he couldn't guess. It must have always been inside of him, but he'd failed to see it. He needed to talk to someone.

Fabian reached for his cell phone, scrolling until he found the one person who he could always be honest with.

Fabian: **Can we meet for a drink tonight?**

The response was immediate.

SweetTina: **Of course. I'm at the restaurant tonight. Meet me there at 8ish?**

Fabian: **See you then.**

At seven-forty-five in the evening, he showed up at L'Atelier where Martina—Sweet Tina—worked as a pastry chef. She'd gotten off early and joined him for drinks at the bar overlooking the massive indoor aquarium with exotic bright colored fish and other odd sea creatures.

"What's that?" Fabian pointed to an eggplant-shaped thing with bright tentacles flaring out.

Martina laughed, taking a sip of her gin martini. "That's what you call a sea cucumber." From the corner of his eye, he knew she was staring at him. He didn't care, though, only continued to drink the same expensive scotch he always did. A light sigh sounded from her lips. "You don't seem okay."

His gaze fell to the bottom of his old fashioned glass. He stared hard into the amber liquid, trying to see the future in the scotch like a fortune-teller. But he certainly wasn't a fortune-teller. Without looking at her, he asked, "What do you think of me?"

She laughed at first, but it faded when she realized he was serious. Her fingers wrapped around his elbow. "What do you mean what do I think of you?"

"Do you think I'm a prick?" He finally met her gaze. "An asshole? A player?" He took a heavier sip that time and continued. "Do you think I use women for sex and break their hearts?"

Martina's mouth opened, and quickly closed. Confusion colored her face pink. He'd asked a big question. Had no idea if he would get an honest answer, but he was ready to hear the truth. She gulped, but not before she removed her hand from his elbow. "You've always been upfront with me about what you want. So, I wouldn't say you're an asshole or a prick."

"That's not really my question, is it?" He was too harsh. Didn't mean to be. His gaze dropped back to his glass of scotch. "I'm sorry."

"Is it Camille?" Martina asked quietly. She'd known about Camille the whole time and continued to see him anyway. Not the other way around, though. Martina was older than Fabian and was much more mature than the other women he *dated*. She never placed an expectation on him, which was precisely why she'd stayed in the rotation the longest. "Did she find out about me? Or someone else."

Or someone else. That burned him inside in a way that Martina would never know. "Do you ever think that maybe I might want just o*ne*? A one?"

"The one?"

"Maybe." He stared for several seconds into the aquarium again. "My dad wants me to stop womanizing and get serious with Camille. And you know why?" He faced her, only seeing a glint of sadness in her eyes, but nothing else on her face suggested she was affected in any way by what he said.

"Why?" Her voice was soft.

"Because her family has connections." He said it as if it was the worst thing to have. Maybe it was. Maybe he didn't want someone because of anything they had. "He thinks that our family could benefit from creating a union with an auto dealer empire."

"What do you think?"

He turned back to his drink. "I think I just wanted to fuck her when it was convenient for me." The words were brusque, but true. He couldn't face Martina for several seconds after he said them.

Silence. Neither spoke for a while. But when Martina spoke, it was in her usual sweet, non-judgmental tone. "You know I'm here for you…"

He grunted to himself. "I can't do that anymore, Tina. I just…" Thoughts of Toni beat the walls of his mind. Infiltrated every crevice inside him. "I can't."

"There's someone else?" Martina caught on quick, and he loved her calmness. Her acceptance. No other woman had given him that before. "A *one*?"

He only nodded and tossed back the rest of his scotch, the warm liquid burning his insides all the way down.

"Who is it?"

They locked gazes. "It's my boss. And I'm probably the worst guy she's ever met."

Her knee knocked his under the bar. "That's not true. You're a wonderful guy. I always enjoy our time together." Fabian knew she was referring to the screwing alone. "Have you tried to get to know her? Without the act I mean. Really know her?"

His ears quirked up. "What act?"

"The 'I'm a womanizer and I can make all these women fall in love with me then I'll reject them because I'm really scared of getting hurt' act."

He sat back against the high stool chair, taking in what she'd just said, and replaying it. It sounded awfully familiar. "Is that what I do?" His words were hollow, just like how he felt inside.

She shrugged. "Just a thought."

"You know what's funny?" His ability to be so candid at that point surprised him, but he wasn't afraid of what it all meant. "If I really got to know her and she really got to know me, I bet she could break me."

"Oh, Fabian. That's … beautiful." A smile stretched her face.

"That's fucking scary."

"I'm afraid that's what it takes." She sounded somber. A look of longing entered her eyes, as if she knew this with the whole of her heart.

"Even when you seriously have no idea how it will all turn out?"

"Well, handsome, that's part of the fun." She winked at him, the sparkle finding her hazel eyes again. Always did.

He fell back in his stool. "Doesn't feel like fun." His twisted insides proved it. Never had he experienced this level of desperation. It was like yearning. Definitely made him feel out of control. He'd always been in control up until now. This wasn't fun. Not even a little bit. And that feeling of "not feeling like fun" hit him in the face when he got an eyeful of Toni walking in with Stephan from across the bar.

Seriously!

His stomach flopped. Why the hell was she with Stephan after everything he did? Fabian shook his head in denial. No way was she really with that jerk. There was just no way she would be with *him.*

"Fabian?" Martina tugged his clenched arm. "What's wrong?"

He couldn't respond. All focus was on Toni. Waiting and willing for her to look his way. "What the hell?" he whispered, growing so anxious he thought he'd explode.

The blood boiled in him. What would he do? Where would he look? He had no idea how to feel about seeing her there with another man. Especially when he had to accept that he wanted her and she didn't want him back.

Walk away. If he didn't leave, Stephan would be on the floor. If that happened, he would ruin his chances with Toni, if he had one, and ruin his chance to be partner at his dad's firm.

Just then, Toni's gaze caught his from across the restaurant. Her eyes grew wide and filled with emotion. Her lips pressed together as her gaze shifted to Stephan. Fabian waited for her to react bigger than that. Stand. Walk to him. Something other than look like a deer caught in a headlight. But she didn't. In fact, she looked away, ignoring him completely. Stephan had been none the wiser, which Fabian was grateful for. But, he couldn't stay and watch her with him.

He stood from the stool, a fire ravaging his insides. "I have to go, Tina. Sorry. I've… I forgot I have to do something." She didn't respond to him, or if she had, Fabian didn't hear. He only heard the blood coursing between his ears until he was outside waiting for the valet to fetch his Bentley. The sounds of lower Montrose grabbed him, making the night seem surreal. How was he supposed to face Toni tomorrow morning when she expected him to deliver her coffee at exactly eight-fifteen and he just wanted to make her his?

* * * *

Her ribs ached. Toni thought her chest might explode. In her peripheral view, she watched Fabian exit the restaurant with haste. And anger, from what she gathered. He was pissed. She knew why. So many thoughts ran through her mind. The battle inside her raged, and for one reason alone. She was affected by him. By what she saw. His reaction to seeing her with Stephan seemed unfounded, yet not. Something was between them. Something she couldn't deny, even as she watched him leave, willing him to come back. To save her again.

"Love, are you okay? You look like you saw a ghost." Stephan's overly white smile showed between his perfect lips on his perfectly proportionate tan face. He was a living Ken doll—blond and all-American golden boy. How had she just realized how much she truly hated him?

"Don't call me that." She twisted the linen cloth over her bare legs. "I'm fine." Major lie. She glanced back to the door, Fabian was out of sight. The need to go after him made her skin itch.

"You didn't say anything during the car ride over here." He tilted his head. "I have to say, I'm glad it's just the two of us."

"I'm not," she muttered under her breath.

Stephan chose to ignore her, obviously. "I won't mention what happened at H Bar with the Pallis kid. I just want to start over. Clean slate. What do you say?"

Was he serious? Did he think he was doing *her* a favor? A string of curse words formed at the tip of her tongue, but she suppressed the need to unleash them. "I say I can never trust you again." Good start. She shifted in her seat, glancing at her phone.

"Fair enough."

Fair enough? Not even close.

He looked up at the approaching waiter. "We'll start with a bottle of Krug if you have it."

"We do." The waiter nodded. "Any particular vintage?"

Stephan glanced to Toni, blinding her with his smile. "The best vintage you have. We're celebrating."

"Very well, sir." The waiter nodded at Toni before he pivoted on his heels away from the table.

"What are we celebrating?" Toni crossed her arms over her abdomen.

"Our ... reunion." He winked that time.

Toni sighed, dropping her gaze. Reminding herself this was all for her mother. "Stephan, I don't think—"

"Helene told you how excited everyone is about us working it out, right? I know she was ecstatic. And being as ill as she is, what else does she have to hold on to other than her only child being united in a fruitful union."

Low blow. She closed her eyelids tight. *One ... two ... three ...* "Fruitful union? What the hell does that mean?"

"It means…" He reached over the small table to take her hands in his. "That we are back together, and we will get engaged again and be married and have children. Hopefully, all before your mother passes."

She snatched her hands away. "You're an asshole," she hissed. "How dare you use my mother against me like this? This is low, Stephan. I can't believe this is who you are. Oh wait, maybe I can believe it."

He grabbed her hands again with force. She winced from the force of it. In a firm voice, he made his declaration. "I love you, Antonia. We will be together again. I'm afraid you have no choice. Our families are expecting this. Are you going to let them down? Let your mother down?"

She turned away. How could she look at him for one more second?

"Besides, you don't know how to be on your own. You're groomed to be a trophy wife. My trophy wife."

The statement knocked the breath right out of her. It's what she always knew. The very idea she began to loathe once she took over for her mom. Trophy wife. That's what she was supposed to be. Someone who had to play a part. Someone who would be known as Stephan's wife.

"Love?" His words were softer, unlike the death grip hold on her hands. "You do see why it's best just to accept this, right? Everyone is happy. Helene is ecstatic."

"Enough," she snapped.

Stephan didn't have an ounce of emotion on his face. "You'll come to your senses soon enough."

She yanked her hands away with all the energy she could manage. "I have to go." Standing, she grabbed her phone and dialed Miles.

Stephan stood as well, following her as she moved between the square cloth-covered tables. "Where are you going?"

"Miles, pick me up at L'Atelier now." She hung up without saying goodbye. Outside, she actually took a breath. But it didn't last as Stephan twirled her around to face him with a hard tug. "Leave me alone, Stephan."

"Where are you going?" Finally, some emotion creased his face. He was livid. The man always hated not getting his way.

"I have to go. I need to think."

"Think about what?" He was too close to her face then. A hard slap would change that, but she didn't have it in her to assault him.

From around the corner, she spotted the

Robuchon Mercedes limo turning down the narrow street. Her penthouse was only a few blocks away.

"Everything."

"I wanted to celebrate tonight." Never did she think he'd lower himself to tantrums when he didn't get his way.

"I have nothing to celebrate." She turned from him just as Miles pulled up.

Stephan followed her. "Maybe I came on too strong. Let me take you to dinner again tomorrow."

Hell no!

Without answering, she opened the door and shut it. "Take me to work."

* * * *

When she got home from the office, she reread the email she'd printed out. The first report to Mr. Pallis regarding his son. Regarding Fabian.

To: Victor Pallis(Victor@PEngineering.biz)

From: Toni Robuchon(t.robuchon@robuchoninvestments.biz)

Date: Tuesday, July 21

RE: Fabian – Week 1

Mr. Pallis –

As requested, I am writing you to report Fabian's progress as my assistant. I've found that he is not experienced in professional behavior in the office. He encourages behavior from female employees that, if continued, could result in reprimanding. In addition, he doesn't take instruction well. At times, I feel he borders on misogynistic behavior. Being under my management, I hope he can learn to respect women as equals and professionals.

I have been lenient on him this first week, as I wanted to get a sense of his personality, but moving forward, I will require he attend training per our Human Resources employee requirements. Specifically, sexual harassment in the workplace. I guarantee you Fabian will learn he doesn't always get his way with women.

Sincerely,
Toni Robuchon
Acting CEO
Robuchon Investments

The whole time she read and reread the email, she could only think about Fabian's mouth on hers. Telling her his deepest secret... She simply couldn't forget.

Chapter Fourteen

"Respect woman as equals and professionals? Are you fucking kidding me?" Fabian stood in the middle of his kitchen, cell phone pressed firmly against his ear to the point of pain. He raked his hand through his already screwed up hair. Everything his father said to him seemed like a joke. He waited for him to say *just kidding*. Unfortunately, his father wasn't much of a jokester. "I can't believe she said that, Dad." Now he was livid. After everything that had happened over the last week, that was what Toni had reported to his father?

"Goddamn it, Fabian!" his father barked into the receiver. "I told you to straighten up. And look, you can't even act right for a week. I'm really ashamed, son. I don't see how I would want you as a partner. Sexually harassing all my female employees? You'll end the company with lawsuits alone!"

"Wow, Dad. That's what you really think of me?" A massive brick smashing into his chest would hurt less. Fabian stumbled back until his butt found the edge of the island counter. None of it could be real. He couldn't wrap his mind around it. No way could Toni actually believe the words she typed to his father.

"It's what you're proving to me, Fabian."

"And you believe what Toni said? That I border on misogynistic behavior?" If anyone bordered on that kind of behavior, it was his father. He was sick with the accusation. He was crushed by it. By her.

"You carry on with women, treating them like garbage. And in public! If you're going to be an ass, Fabian, I need you to do it outside the public eye. You know we have a reputation in this town."

"Is that why Mom left us?" The question came

135

out of him as if it had been on the tip of his tongue, waiting for the right moment. The words from his own mouth surprised him.

Silence. Of course, there would be. Fabian recalled the conversation he'd had with his father twenty years ago about his mother. *She's never coming back.* He'd never forget that day. Even though he was only six, he should never have had to lose the one woman who is supposed to love him forever.

"You don't know anything about it." His father's voice was low, telling of how much he contained himself. It was a definitive statement, but not enough to stop Fabian. He wasn't that six-year-old boy anymore.

With a tone meant to rival his father's, he said, "Then tell me." Fabian waited, his whole body shook with adrenaline.

Fabian's father dismissed him, as usual. "All you need to know is she left." Something told Fabian there was much more to it than that.

"Do mothers leave their sons?" He closed his eyes, warmed by the swell of unshed tears.

"She left and she died, Fabian. What does this have to do with anything?" His words were too matter-of-fact. Nothing to show he ever cared about Danika Pallis. But it was the only thing Fabian cared about.

"Everything." Fabian couldn't continue, only ended the call. He promptly tossed the phone across the room, hoping to break the damn thing.

Misogynist? No way. He was a lot of things, but not that. Not even close. With the thought ripe in his mind, he marched over to his phone again, relieved it didn't break. Also relieved—and not surprised—his father didn't bother to call him back. He scrolled through his contacts until he settled upon Antonia Robuchon, who he'd labeled "SexyBossLady". He frowned. With swift fingers, he selected the edited button and deleted the sentiment, replacing SexyBossLady with Antonia Robuchon.

He stared at her name. Stared so hard he could see the pixels. The whys were getting to him. Why would Toni say that? Why would Toni kiss him? Why would Toni say she couldn't like a man like him? Why would Toni have anything to do to with her ex? Why would Toni act like she didn't want Fabian as much she he wanted her? Why couldn't she just…

Goddamn it. He didn't like where his mind was going. All the women in his life flashed before him. Camille. Martina. Countless others he'd forgotten. He rubbed his face, dragging a tear down to his chin. Only his mother could soothe him in that moment. Of that he was sure.

Call her. Don't call her. He couldn't convince himself of either. What would he say? Demand an explanation? He dropped the phone on the couch and dropped himself against it too. The cushions caught his full weight. Another sigh blew passed his lips.

How could he face her in the office? Fabian picked up his phone, but not to call Toni. He needed to be as far away from her as possible.

Fabian: **Captain, get her ready. I want to depart Kemah at 0800.**

Moments later a text lit the screen.

Captain Norway: **Yes sir. Winds not favorable, FYI.**

Fabian: **I don't care. I need to be on the Gulf ASAP.**

Captain Norway: **As you wish.**

As he wished? Not even close.

* * * *

The evening's events replayed in Toni's mind.

She lay on her bed, looking at her phone multiple times, reading and rereading the email she sent to Mr. Pallis. Regret came strong, though at first, it was pure panic and desperation. Lies, all lies. She didn't believe any of the things she said about Fabian. He wasn't a misogynist. More likely, he was the opposite. He loved women too much, and that was her problem with him. After he found about the report, he would have a big problem with her.

Manipulation wasn't her strong suit—she wasn't Stephan. She wasn't good at it, obviously. Fabian would know right away she was lying. He always seemed to know. But how else would she keep him? That was her intention. Keep him in the office. *God, I'm a horrible person*. She dropped her face against her palms, groaning. Maybe she should just recall the email. Mr. Pallis couldn't possibly have read it already.

She studied her phone, hesitating before she opened the email application. Recalling the email was the right thing to do. It would be a miracle if it was still an option. As much as she wanted to, she just couldn't do it.

What am I afraid of?

She'd never been so scared to do something. Act on something. Before she could gather the strength to make an actual move, the phone vibrated with an incoming email. She jumped up to a sitting position. Victor Pallis's name popped up in bold letters on the screen. *Oh God!*

Thump. Thump. Thump. Her heart beat inside her head, shaking her with each pulse. She would have to read the email. No way around it. She'd made her bed, despite not considering what would happen if her plan completely backfired. Fabian could quit. Mr. Pallis could sever the agreement. Fabian could be gone. Completely the opposite of what she wanted of course. The courage to read the email took at least ten minutes to come.

To: Toni Robuchon(t.robuchon@robuchoninvestments.biz)
From: Victor Pallis(Victor@PEngineering.biz)
Date: Tuesday, July 21
RE: RE: Fabian – Week 1
Miss Robuchon –
I am extremely disappointed to hear Fabian's behavior has been less than acceptable. I will speak with him about this immediately. Should he not correct the issues you have described by next week, I will remove him from your employment.
Sincerely,
Victor Pallis
President, Managing Partner
Pallis Engineering

Oh God! Exactly what she was afraid of. Now, she had the inevitable confrontation with Fabian to look forward to. Tomorrow. How would she prepare for that disaster? To add insult to injury, another message popped up on her screen.

Stephan Bradley: **Hi <3. Spoke with Helene & she and I decided I should go into the office this week. I can't wait to spend my day with you. Kiss. SB.**

Toni gritted her teeth until they hurt. Too much. Everything was too much. Had she stepped into some awful reality show? She missed the days when she isolated herself in her penthouse with only a yoga class to look forward to. When did it all get so complicated? She looked back the unwanted message, denying her initial reaction to respond in anger. Stephan knew exactly how to get to her. She couldn't engage with him. Instead, she called her mother.

"Toni, it's late. Are you all right?" The alarm in her mother's weak voice made Toni regret she called. But she simply couldn't allow her mother and Stephan to make life plans for her anymore.

"Sorry, Mom. I know it's after ten. But I really have to talk to you." A pause followed, and her heart pounded ten-fold.

"Well, what it is?" Nothing could stop her mother's ability to get her annoyance across, not even chemotherapy. "Is this about that startup you're trying to push for investment? You're not experienced enough to suggest what is a good investment, Antonia."

Toni bit her bottom lip. She gazed at the decorative scroll print on her comforter to maintain her sanity. "No, it's about Stephan."

"What about him?"

Now that she had her mother's undivided attention, Toni struggled to find the words. All her life, she'd been intimidated by her mother. Though she always let it go, she really hated that her mother treated her like she was still a child. "I don't want him in the office. Fabian is more than capable. He has two very advanced degrees, you know. And he's helped me understand some bio technologies that, by the way, no one else here understands. He's also made some great recommendations."

Her mother scoffed. "He's an annoyance and I only agreed to hire him because of my relationship with Victor. But, that feckless kid won't be there for long."

"Mom." All her anger centered on that one word. It surprised her—and her mother.

Her mother sighed into the receiver. The silence lingered until her mother refocused her anger. "I didn't get a very promising report from the doctor."

Toni squeezed her eyes shut. Immediately, she was filled with guilt. Were her issues really that important compared to her mother's life? "What do you mean?"

"Therapy isn't working as well as they hoped. And I feel myself getting sicker, weaker, every day." She paused again. Longer that time and Toni would've burst into tears if she wasn't holding her breath. "I really don't know how much longer. Less than six months, I'm assuming."

The phone slipped through Toni's fingers. The shock immobilized her, made her completely still, lifeless. She couldn't blink away the tears that formed and ran down her cheeks. The ache in her chest grew and grew until she folded over in a fetal position. Muffled sounds came out of the receiver on the bed. She lifted it to her ear with haste.

"Yes, Mom?"

"That's why I want you and Stephan to follow through with the plans you'd had. I want to know you'll be okay and married to a capable man from an exceptional family. And I want your husband to be CEO of RI."

And just like that she was six years old again. Her voice just as small as it was back then. "Why can't I be CEO of RI?"

"Oh, honey, you're not suited for work."

"But I have an MBA from Rice."

"And it was money well spent." Her mother paused again. "Antonia, dear, you always knew your path. Now seems like the perfect time."

The lump in Toni's throat made it impossible to speak, but she stormed through the pain somehow. "But you're leaving me."

"We all leave sometime, don't we?"

In a whisper, Toni agreed, "Yes."

Chapter Fifteen

Fabian walked through the Robuchon Investments lobby with a dark tan and a bone to pick with Toni. He also had a paper cup of coffee—three packets of cane sugar and fat-free organic milk—incidentally. Two days out on the Gulf was what he needed. Everything he could possibly obsess about, he did. Now, he was ready to confront her. He walked out of the elevator, thinking about the email for the zillionth time. Misogynist? He would *not* let that go. Even if he was already fired for not showing up or calling the two days he was away, she needed to hear him out.

Davina stood at the reception desk, beaming at him. "Fabian!" Her eyes glittered under the track lighting overhead. "We thought you quit." She slid her palm up her hip until it landed at her waist. "I'm glad you didn't."

"I'm probably fired." He chuckled half-heartedly. Davina dropped her hand from her hip.

"You're probably fired?" Toni's voice sounded from behind him. His stomach rippled. God, he wanted to see her. He missed her. He wanted to stare in her eyes, but he didn't. Instead, he watched Davina scurry to her chair.

"Am I?" Feeling the weight of her glower on his back, Fabian turned slowly until she came into full view, ready to face her. Black t-strap Louboutins. Slicked back ponytail. Eyes lined into striking almonds. Is it possible that this woman could be more beautiful than he last remembered? His plan to confront her right away might be shattered.

Her perfectly arched eyebrow lifted. "You've been gone two days without so much as a call or an email." Her eyes remained hard, and he wondered if she was truly mad he didn't contact her.

His gaze zeroed in on her lips. Soft. Plump. He couldn't stop thinking about kissing her again, even though he wanted to be indignant about what she emailed his father. But those lips ... he could probably overlook everything just to feel those lips on his. To part them with his tongue.

"Well..." Fabian trailed off just as Stephan Bradley entered the lobby and quickly moved next to Toni, placing his hand on her waist.

His stomach flopped. Even though Toni backed away from Stephan, she didn't soften toward Fabian. Fabian didn't like how close Stephan was to her. What the hell was going on?

"Well?" she demanded.

Walk away. Forget it all. Fabian didn't want to listen to the voice in his head. No way could he walk away or forget it. Not after spending two days thinking about nothing else. His gaze dropped to his Prada shoes, taking in the perfecting stitching, thinking of what he would say next. He met Toni's eyes. "We need to talk."

"Yes, we do," she agreed curtly.

"We can meet in the conference room," Stephan interjected.

"This doesn't concern you, Bradley," Fabian barked, the rush of anger heating him exponentially. Stephan shouldn't affect him that much. In actuality, he was irrelevant to Fabian. But if Toni was with him again... No, he couldn't think of that.

Stephan stepped toward him only to be stopped by Toni's hand. "I'll handle this." To Fabian, she said, "Go to the small conference room. I'll be there in a few minutes."

In the conference room, he paced the length of the table, at times glancing out of the picturesque window displaying downtown. His hand still around Toni's coffee, he sipped the cooling liquid, grimacing at the sweetness. *God, that's awful.* He really hated her taste in coffee. And ex-fiancés. Promptly, he tossed it in the trash near the door. Five minutes might have passed, or five hours. He couldn't tell which. Whichever it was, it seemed like an eternity before Toni stood on the other side of the glass door. Their eyes met.

The air changed the moment she stepped into the room. Her sweet perfume scented the space, and he breathed in, finding his defenses had already been dismantled. Clenching his jaw, he met her half way. His heart skipped a beat once he wasn't quite a foot from her.

Her mouth quirked. "Looks like you've been vacationing in the Caribbean."

"Just the Gulf, but I wouldn't call it vacationing."

Her eyes lowered to his mouth, quickly snapping back up. Still, she didn't step away from him. "You can't just leave a job, Fabian."

"And you can't lie."

Her eyes widened, before quickly narrowing to slits. "I don't."

"Don't you?" Then she stepped back.

In response, he stepped forward. No way was she walking away from him. Not after everything that had happened between them. "I'm a misogynist?"

She gripped the back of the nearest chair tucked under the gargantuan table.

His resolve to let her have it grew again. He would have to overlook how much he wanted to lay her on the table and put her ankles on his shoulders. "I know what you told my father." She looked away. "Look at me, Antonia. Is that what you really think?"

She smoothed down the front of her white fitted dress as if only to distract herself from the truth he needed her to say. "I-I only meant—"

"After everything that's happened between us, how could you say that to my father, of all people?"

Toni avoided his stare. "I know you helped me, and I am grateful. Please don't think I'm not."

"And what about what happened in your office? Your lips on mine, my hand in your panties. It seems to me you wouldn't let a misogynist do that to you. Or am I wrong?" He'd thought of Stephan then, and it made him sick.

"Stop it, please."

"I can't stop it. Not with you." His body swayed, searching for stability. For the first time he felt the angst of desperation and knew he would forgive her in a heartbeat.

She spun toward him, determination set in her eyes. "You have to stop it." When Fabian didn't—couldn't—respond, she continued, "Misogynist was wrong. I shouldn't have said that. I'm sorry. I will email your father immediately."

"You're not going to tell me why you lied? You won't at least give me that?" Her eyes darkened with the emotions inside her. He could see them as clear as he felt his own emotions welling up inside him.

"I know you want to get out of here as fast as I want you gone."

Her words stabbed him, leaving him winded.

Fine. He straightened and backed away from her, not ignoring the inflection in her eyes. "Fire me then."

* * * *

"You can quit." *Please don't.*

He grunted. "Do you want me to?"

She worried her lips together. "Well, it's not the agreement your father made with my mother."

"What isn't?"

"That you quit." Toni looked at her hands, which she had clasped together against her stomach. "You can't prove to your father you're capable if you quit."

"Oh, you care about that?"

"Fabian." All her lies came back to bite her in the ass. She wanted to tell him the truth. Her truth. But the longer she looked into his tormented eyes, the more she realized she could never tell him why. Clearing her throat, she took a step closer to him, feeling how powerful his body was. What pull he had on her. "I want to honor their agreement. And I want you to be a partner at your dad's company."

He rubbed his forehead, the confusion in his eyes mirroring what she felt inside. "I don't understand you, Toni. At all. None of this makes sense." None of it made sense to her.

"I'm sorry." She didn't know what else to say.

He glowered. "Why do you keep telling me nothing except 'I'm sorry'?"

"Because I am." Out of shame, she looked away. She didn't deserve to look at him. "About everything."

"About us?"

She nodded her head. "Especially that." She met his gaze again, knowing her words hurt him.

"Is that why Stephan is here?" In a few wide strides, he was close to her again. So close. Her pulse thumped at her throat. Each one bordered on painful. She wanted him so desperately … yet, she was scared. He asked again in her silence, "Is it?"

She nodded.

His eyes emptied, as did her heart. It was so silent, a pin drop could fall and make a crashing sound. They stared at each other as if it were the last time. Maybe it would be the last time. Everything they had up until that point was gone. The shared deep secrets. The kisses she couldn't forget. All gone.

Toni moved away from him, opening the glass door. She needed to leave. "So business as usual then?"

"Whatever you say, boss."

* * * *

At the end of the day, Toni grew increasingly anxious. She'd left Fabian in the conference room and hadn't spoken to him since. At least a dozen times she went to his door, lifting her fist to knock. She wanted to tell him the truth about everything. Her feelings for him. Why Stephan was really in the office. Her dying mother. She didn't. In the midst of her thoughts, the man she loathed more than her lies stood in her office doorway. He beamed at her as if all was well with the world. As if the world was his oyster. She grunted at the sight, because it was, always was.

"What do you want, Stephan?"

He strolled over to the chair across her desk. "I wanted to talk about the gala tomorrow. I spoke to Helene and we've agreed that you and I will arrive as a couple. It's time Houston society knew we are back together and soon to be engaged."

In quick reaction, she crossed her arms over her chest. "You will not speak to my mother about anything anymore. You need something, you ask me. Got it?" Her strength exhilarated her.

Stephan narrowed his gaze, also surprised it would seem. "Once we're married, I won't tolerate this attitude. It's your mother's wish and you, of all people, should respect it. She's dying, for God's sake."

Toni bit her tongue. She wanted to scream. Stephan knew exactly how to get his way. Involve her *dying* mother? That was too cruel. Toni couldn't fathom why people like that lived in the world. She'd been too sheltered her whole life.

The words were like acid on her tongue. "You know I'm doing this for my mother."

Something sinister tainted his wide smile. "I know."

"You also know I don't want you. Not even a little bit." She pressed her lips together. Hating him more would be impossible. But every second that went by proved it was possible.

"Oh, because you want that loser Pallis?" He smirked. "I'm really doing you a favor. He'll just fuck you and leave like he's known to do."

"You don't know him," she barked, immediately averting her gaze to papers on her desk.

A few beats of silence passed before Stephan responded. "I'll pick you up at six. We'll attend the sponsor dinner as well."

When she looked up again, he was gone.

After two hours of hardcore yoga, she waited for Miles in the front of the studio. It had been a rough class, with the remnants of her conversation with Stephan still playing on a loop in her mind. How was she going to get out of this engagement? Family duty wasn't for the faint of heart she quickly realized, and began to hate her family status like she never had. Wealth had been something she'd thought she would always need. A trust fund to spend on whatever her heart desired. But what if what she desired didn't cost anything … except her mother's acceptance? She stilled with the sobering thought.

A breeze kissed her faced as she looked up again. The loud roaring engine caught her full attention as a matte black convertible Ferrari raced into the parking lot. Toni was even more distracted by the long black hair whipping from the passenger's seat. The driver turned down the front of the yoga studio. When she saw the driver's face, her whole body froze. *Fabian*.

He stopped in front of her. "Hey, boss," he called from the driver's seat, facing her. "Fancy seeing you here."

Toni glanced to the brunette sitting pretty in the bucket seat with a smirk on her lips. *Camille*. Her stomach flopped again and all the balance she tried to find in yoga class collapsed. "You really are flashy, aren't you, Fabian?" She could barely get the words out.

"You don't like flashy?" Fabian asked, brooding.

"No, I don't," she said, fighting through the largest lump in her throat she'd ever had. From afar, she spotted Miles turning the corner. *Oh, God, please hurry*. She willed Miles to rescue her. Though she didn't want to, she glanced at Camille—perfect Camille—again, her heart dropping. On the approach, she rushed to the curb, grabbed the handle to the limo door and pulled it open before Miles had fully stopped. She dove into the back with her yoga mat tight under her arm. "Home, Miles. Now!"

Anger and jealousy were the first emotions to bubble up. To see Fabian with another woman made her sick. She shut her eyes, hoping to forget what she saw. Then the disappointment followed. She thought she'd been wrong about him. How could he say he wanted her and then so quickly have someone else? Irrational as it might seem, because she'd rejected him, he should not be with another woman. But he was a playboy, after all. Playboys always had another woman.

"Are you all right, Miss Robuchon?" Miles asked, gazing at her through the rearview mirror.

Toni lifted her fingers to her cheeks, touching fallen tears. Once the limo moved passed the stop sign, she said, "No, Miles. I'm not all right. But I'll pretend that I am."

Chapter Sixteen

Fabian decided something, half-heartedly. Because he didn't have a choice. He'd decided to take Camille to the gala on Saturday. Nothing else. Not a date. Not a sex-filled night afterward. Nothing. He couldn't even Netflix-and-chill with her the night before as he set out to, which was his move. At any rate, he'd told her the deal right up front, which she seemed more than happy to oblige.

Fabian gazed in the mirror as he tied the checkered bow tie at his throat. It wasn't quite right. With a grunt, he unraveled the bow. Nothing was quite right. He'd been too hyper-focused on Toni to concentrate. He was still mad as hell with her. Her lies and her obvious backtracking. What the hell was going on? Really, he was more mad at himself for not forcing it out of her—assuming he could. Maybe it didn't matter anymore. Stephan was in the picture again. The thought made Fabian want to explode. How could Toni let *him* in her life again? He couldn't bring himself to believe she would fall for Stephan again.

"Here, let me try." Camille came up behind him. His eyes met hers. Such admiration in them—misplaced admiration. He wished she didn't see the world in him.

"Thanks." He grazed the lush material of his suit as he dropped his hands. All his suits were tailor made. Nothing feigned confidence like a well-fitted suit. Though he usually had confidence out nose, he needed a bit of help that day. Camille worked quickly. She was so close to him—unnecessarily close. He could do anything he wanted to her. Touch her. Kiss her. Bend her over. But all his desires for Camille were gone. Someone else had them. And he would see her at the gala with her ex.

"You look distant, Fabian."

True, he couldn't be farther from her. Fabian shook his head, glancing back to the full-length mirror just as she finished tying the bow tie. She stepped away so he could take in her handy work. "Good job." She lifted on her toes to kiss him, annoyed when he only kissed her cheek. Just like the night before when they streamed movies in his condo, he couldn't as much as put his arm around her. How could he do anything when he'd just seen Toni in her yoga outfit? Looking beautiful. And so unavailable.

"Thank you." She turned in her white nothing of a cocktail dress.

Fabian looked at himself again. Ready to face the Pallis Engineering Gala Sponsors dinner. That meant seeing his father. Fabian frowned. They hadn't left their last phone conversation on great terms, but when did they ever? "God, the old man will surely be unbearable tonight. I hope the bastard doesn't embarrass the family." Ironically, his father always accused *him* of embarrassing the family.

"We should go."

In his Bentley, he blasted Arvo Part. It always calmed him just before a big event, especially one that included his father. His senses were heightened, though, with all the uncertainly he would soon walk into. He had to mentally prepare to see Toni and Stephan. Fabian tapped a finger against the steering wheel as he drove down to the Halman Hotel, owned by his friend Dallas's family. They'd generously donated the ballroom for the gala every year for as long as Fabian could remember.

"You're really nervous to see your dad, aren't you?" Camille rubbed his thigh.

And Toni. "I just need a drink. I'll be fine."

Inside the Halman Hotel, Fabian stopped Camille

just before the entrance to the smaller ballroom. "Remember I told you we're not here together as a couple."

A ripple of emotion passed over her face. "I know you need time."

"Right…" He sighed, scanning the area and recognizing many faces. Dallas, Ty, and Konrad had taken up the area near the bar. Before he could complete his sentence, he saw her. *Toni.* She stood at the far end of the dining area, dressed like a mermaid in a fitted sea foam green dress that kissed the floor with its length. The neck plunged far, but not indecently far, down her chest, hinting at her small perky breasts. He gulped hard. Long dark hair curled over one shoulder and the rest was pinned up on the opposite side. Every time she turned her head to greet someone, sparkling diamond earrings caught the light as they dangled, nearly touching her shoulders.

"Is that your boss?" Camille stepped in front of him, a scowl on her face.

He swallowed. "That's Antonia Robuchon, all right." They both stared at her. What would Toni think about seeing him with Camille again? He hoped she didn't get the wrong idea about her.

"How much longer are you going to be working for her?"

He ignored her question because Toni had his full attention. She mesmerized him. Stephan hadn't been pinned at her side like Fabian would expect him to be. *Is she alone?* Before he could make a move or say something else, Toni met his gaze from across the room. She froze. It was like a scene in a movie. But, they weren't lovers, and she didn't want anything to do with him. Toni narrowed her eyes when as she shifted her gaze to Camille. His heart thumped. She didn't like what she saw. Camille next to him. But she didn't give him a chance to indicate that he and Camille weren't together. Instead, Toni turned away without acknowledging him.

Damn.

"Let's go mingle," he said to Camille over his shoulder as he headed toward his friends.

Camille followed at his heels, pulling him to a halt. "Here." She handed him a champagne flute and took a sip of her own. "I wish they were serving something better."

"This is fine with me." He tossed it back just as his friends walked over. Someone else walked over too. Toni.

"You should take it easy with that, Mr. Pallis. I don't want anyone thinking my employee is an alcoholic or a—"

"Misogynist," he finished her sentence, holding her glower with his own. He'd began to feel irritated at her. If anyone should be annoyed, it was him. But she was so beautiful... He was convinced he needed to get to the bottom of her lie and why Stephan was hanging around. Something wasn't adding up.

"This tosser is a load of things, but I don't think a misogynist is one of them," Konrad chimed in, chuckling. Dallas and Ty laughed. All eyes on Toni.

Toni nodded at the guys. "Hello. Nice to see you again."

The guys said their hellos, all feeling the chill coming from Camille who stared at Toni for way too long to be friendly.

"Looks like we need another drink, lads," Konrad said, tossing a sympathetic glance to Fabian who didn't know how the Camille/Toni meeting would go. The fewer spectators the better.

"Come to the Halman table. I got prime seats for

you," Dallas said as the three friends left the scene.

Toni made the first move. "Hi, Camille. Lovely to see you. Again." Toni reached out to shake her hand. Camille hesitated before she took it in an awkward handshake.

Smugly, Camille said, "Nice to see you, too. Fabian didn't tell me you do yoga in his complex."

"It's really just a coincidence. I've been going there for at least a year now."

Fabian's chest tightened. He needed to get Toni alone. Everything he wanted to say to her in the conference room was bubbling up in his mind. The words were ready to spill from his tongue.

Ringing bells sounded throughout the dining area. Fabian's father stood near the head of the table holding a glass of champagne. "A quick word, everyone." The crowd settled and he continued. "Thank you so much for sponsoring the Museum of Fine Arts Gala. Without your contributions, this event wouldn't happen, and Pallis Engineering is honored to have you join our yearly pre-Gala Sponsors dinner here at Halman Hotel. So thank you for coming!" The crowd cheered and clapped for several seconds. "And a huge thank you to my personal friends, the Halmans, for allowing us to use this beautiful hotel for this event. With that said, please find your seating assignment. L'Atelier will begin the six-course meal shortly." Another burst of claps and cheers sounded.

"*Bon appétit*," Toni said, just as she turned away from Fabian.

"Toni, wait," Fabian called to her, carelessly taking her arm in his hand. Both women's sets of eyes zeroed in on where he'd touched Toni.

From behind, that deep annoying voice sounded and Toni's arm tensed. "Is there a problem here?"

Stephan.

Toni continued to glare at Fabian. "No problem at all."

He'd released her arm, and noticed Stephan's hand replaced his, but Toni yanked away from him. Fabian watched them walk toward the long dinner table. No way was she with Stephan again. An idiot could see there was nothing between those two. This renewed Fabian's hope, and urgency to get her alone.

"You like her." Camille's accusation was spot on.

He didn't deny it because he couldn't. The silence spoke for him as he led Camille to the special Halman table.

* * * *

"How was Fabian this week?" Mr. Pallis nearly rammed his bulbous belly into Toni. The dinner ended and the gala was in full swing.

"Mr. Pallis!" Toni flinched, her grip tightening around her martini glass, though a good bit spilled over the side on her fingers. "Hello."

"He's been gone—" Stephan came up from behind her only to be cut off.

"Go get me another drink." She shoved the martini glass onto the lapel of his designer suit, spilling vodka all over him. With a few choice words, Stephan took the glass and turned on his heels toward the bar. By the looks of the line, it could be a while.

"You are a sight." Mr. Pallis's dark eyes, unlike Fabian's bright green eyes, dragged over her. He took a hefty gulp of whiskey or scotch perhaps. "Look just like your mother."

Her body warmed. Up until that point, she'd been secure in her dress, quite proud of it. But Mr. Pallis's stare made her feel like she might as well be naked. Toni struggled with a smile. "Thank you."

"How is Helene? I haven't heard from her in

nearly a month." His breath smelled of alcohol. Not to mention the waver in his stance. He might have had more than enough alcohol.

In that second, Toni had never been more grateful to see a scantily clad woman throw herself at a man she had been talking to. A young woman lunged onto Mr. Pallis, squealing as she did so, and proceeded to cover the side of his face with kisses. Red lips trailed down the side of his face.

Toni averted her gaze to the display, it was painful to watch. Fabian walked across the ballroom, clearly disgusted from what he saw. His father liplocked with a woman less than half his age. Her heart ached for Fabian. She only could imagine what it must have been like for Fabian to grow up with a man like Mr. Pallis. He definitely wasn't going to win a dad-of-the-year award anytime soon.

"Mother is doing fine." She did her best to ignore that they'd still been making out in front of her and for all to see. "I actually would like to talk to you about something. It's regarding your son's report…"

He parted from the woman. "Oh?"

"Uh, yes…" Toni glanced at the woman who glared at her for taking away Mr. Pallis's attention. "It's a p-private matter."

"What is a private matter?" Fabian's voice startled her, his fingers curved over her shoulder. He'd touched her every chance he got thus far, and she didn't hate it. Actually, she craved it.

"I want to speak to your father, Fabian." Toni's body coursed with the energy of being close to him again. Though she wanted him near, she knew it would be best if he stayed away from her. Far away. And how could he bring Camille to the gala? Toni moved away, his fingers slipping from her. "We'll speak later, Mr. Pallis. Excuse me."

"You can call me Victor, sweetheart." Mr. Pallis winked.

She'd never seen Fabian frown that hard. What was he thinking?

Doesn't matter. I need to get out of here. With a deep breath, she moved toward the bathrooms. She'd never walked that fast in five-inch heels before.

The gala was not the time to sort out her drama with Fabian, albeit caused by her. God, she really hated herself. Hated how much she'd made a mess of things. But Fabian affected her so tremendously, she couldn't control herself. She was wild with the thought of his fingers on her shoulder. All their other encounters came back to her, leaving her weak and breathless. She was hot with the memories. Intending to get the hell out of there, she entered the dark hall to leading to the ladies' room and was spun around by a strong hand.

She gasped. "Fabian."

His green eyes glowed in that dim hall. His jaw clenched with some attempt to control what was raging inside him. She knew that control. It kept her from throwing herself at him, kissing him, or doing something else her body craved. Raw energy sizzled between them. When he backed her against the wall, she knew it was over for her.

"Goddamn it, Antonia, tell me the truth." His voice was low and growling, like he'd let his animal instincts take over. It scared her a little, but excited her just the same.

She trembled. "So you're with Camille again, are you? Or is she just a friends-with-benefits thing?" Her jealousy showed its ugly head. That she tipped her hand enough to show him such an emotion irked her.

"I'm not with her." He palmed her throat. The soft

pad of his thumb lay on her pulse as it raced. "And don't change the subject. You owe it to me. Tell me why you lied to my father," he demanded softer that time, leaning closer to her face.

Desire worked through her body, igniting her senses. "I… I…" She moaned, acutely aware of how close his mouth was to hers. All she wanted was his lips on her lips. His lips on every part of her.

"Tell me, Toni." His fingers tightened on her throat. She gasped at the eroticism of being caged by him, demanded by him. Her clitoris throbbed with how turned on she was by his power.

And without thinking, the words came. "Because I don't want you to go."

His mouth crashed down on hers. He bit her lips, sucked her tongue and tangled it with his. They matched intensities, both taking exactly what they wanted. She took it all. His lips, his tongue, his touch. He slid his hand down to her sex and rubbed hard until she pushed away in fear of orgasming right there in the hallway.

"We can't," she croaked, trying to get her bearings, only finding the room was spinning faster with each blink.

Fabian pulled her against him. "Don't run from me."

She jerked away from him. "You don't get it."

"Oh, I get it." He scrubbed the side of his head in exasperation. "Admit it, Toni. Admit I might be the one you want."

"What kind of a fool would I have to be to admit that to you?" A spike of anger rose inside her at the thought of Camille and all the other women in his life. "The last thing I'll ever be is your fool." But she wanted to be, horrifically. She wanted him in the worst way for the worst reasons. She wanted to be his fool, his stupid fool who showed up at his place of employment and nagged about a future. She wanted to be just like the others. And that was plain stupid.

"You have no idea what you would be to me." His eyes glistened with the words.

"And I'm not going to find out either." She turned on her heel, reeling in what had just happened between them. Again. She ached deep within, regretting walking away, but knowing she'd regret it more if she stayed.

Chapter Seventeen

At Camille's family River Oaks home, Fabian parked the Bentley in the circular driveway. They'd left the gala early. He was reeling, frustrated, and angry. Confused might be the better word. Way more confused than he was before. And, as much as he didn't want to feel it, sad. The delusion that he could have Toni in some way had collapsed, leaving him with nothing but the numbness of acceptance.

Camille smiled *that* smile when she wanted him in her bed. "Are you coming in?"

He shook his head. "No, I'm not."

She frowned. He didn't know a woman who hated rejection as much as she did. Why wouldn't she? No other man rejected her. Camille could have anyone she wanted. He only wished she didn't want him. She brushed her forehead with the tip of her index finger. "Why not?"

He hung his head a moment, gathering his thoughts. "Because you should have more."

Her blue eyes narrowed. "What?"

"I could go in, fuck you and make you come until you lose your voice. But that's all I would be giving you and you should have more than that." Crude as usual, but he finally was honest with her. She deserved it.

Camille's forehead creased as the realization sank in. By the time she spoke, her eyes glittered with unshed tears. "I can give you time, Fabes. I can wait for you."

He shook his head with a sigh. "No. Don't wait or you'll wait forever and hate me more."

"I can't hate you." She choked on her words.

"But you should." He averted his gaze. All the women he'd used should hate him. Even Sweet Tina.

"Please…" Her voice was a painful whisper.

"I'm not the one for you, Camille. I'm just not." His gaze met hers.

In the smallest, most achingly painful voice, she said, "I wish I never met you." But he couldn't say "sorry" before she practically jumped out and slammed the car door, never looking back at him as she marched up the steps to her father's house and slammed the front door.

He sighed. It was for the best. He continued home, knowing he'd finally done the right thing.

Each step from the elevator to his condo took effort. The kind of effort that involved dragging a sack full of concrete bricks behind him. His heart pounded in his ears as he turned the corner to his wing of the building. What he saw winded him completely. He thought his knees would buckle.

Toni, still in her cocktail gown, sat in front of his door. She stood the moment she saw him, no smile on her face. Uncertainty filled her eyes. From the short distance, he heard the breath surge between her lips.

"I'm a liar."

He didn't speak, only moved into action. He felt light as air as he advanced toward her, drumming up all the energy he had as he lifted her, pressing his mouth on hers hard enough to feel the pain of his desire. She wrapped her legs around his waist. Somehow he was able to get into his condo with Toni in his arms, still kissing her.

In the door to his bedroom, she spoke, her lips on his, tongue teasing him. "I was told to stay away from you."

After biting her lip, he replied, "I was told you're off-limits."

"Take off my dress." She moaned the second he

dropped her on the massive bed. She flipped over, exposing the zipper along the seam of her dress.

"You're gorgeous." He filled his palms with her perfectly plump ass, squeezing hard until she cried out. He found the hem of her dress and slipped his hand under to touch her smooth skin, while his other hand ran up to the back of her head, embedding in her hair. He wanted to caress all of her. Suck and lick all of her. He wanted everything with her.

One kiss after the other, his lips trailed down her back with each inch he'd unzipped her dress. He reveled in her smooth skin, taking in her vanilla scent until his lungs stretched to capacity as he covered her with his breath and touch. She moaned, urging and completely compliant. She wanted him, and he honestly couldn't believe it was all happening. If it was a dream, he would deserve the cruelty of it. But he silently prayed it was real. That she was really there, under him, letting him kiss her, touch her. Allowing him to make her feel like she deserved. Adored. Because he did adore her.

Fabian slipped a hand under her, hiking it up to her breast. And then he flipped her. She yelped. "Fabian!"

"You have no idea what I want to do to you, Toni. None." He yanked at her dress, peeling the silk from her body like it wasn't worth a few thousand dollars he knew it was. He'd buy her another one. As many dresses as she wanted. In nothing but a glittering G-string, she looked at him. "It's like a tiara. Like a princess." She laughed at his ridiculous words, but she was a princess to him. His focus would be one thing alone. Remind his neighbors who lived there.

"I like flashy things," she said low in her throat, the look in her eyes making him harder than he'd ever been.

"So do I." He lowered his head to her stomach, nipping as he trailed down to her princess panties. He slipped a finger under the material at her hipbone and yanked until they tore off. "But you already knew that."

"Oh God, Fabian!" She parted her thighs, showing him everything.

A sigh came out of him. Beautiful didn't describe what she was, laying there on display. She was magical. Heavenly. No word would do her justice. Their eyes met. *Pace yourself.* He wanted it to last. He wanted to give her pleasure she'd never had before. He wanted to be the best she'd ever had.

"What man would leave this?" He spoke mostly to himself, gazing at her body. With both hands, he spread her thighs farther apart. He'd never been so hard in his life. But he didn't want to undress yet. He wanted to focus on her.

"Take your clothes off," she said, reaching for his shirt. Thankfully, he'd left his suit jacket in the car.

He shook his head. "Not yet." He dipped down to her most private part and tasted her there with his lips, and then his tongue.

* * * *

Fabian did it again. He brought her to pleasure quick and hard. Toni moaned at the rising tension inside her. The faster he darted his tongue over her clitoris, the faster her moans turned into cries until the final release quieted her. But for only a moment.

"Oh, God!" she choked, grabbing handfuls of his hair. "Fabian..." She could barely speak.

He lifted his head, revealing a crazed look in his eyes. He wasn't done with her. He stripped off his shirt, barely getting his bow tie off first. The belt came next with clumsy precision. Toni held her breath until he was down to his boxer briefs, the outline of his cock both frightening her and turning her on more if that were possible.

He reached for her, lifting her until they both sat on bent knees before each other. "I can't stay away from you, Toni. I don't know my limits with you. But I want to go all the way." His eyes filled with enough emotion to knock the words out of her mind. She needed to breathe, or else she'd suffocate from his magnetism.

Kissing him was her response. What if tomorrow was different? What if tomorrow never came? She didn't want to think about his words. No, she just wanted him. Crashing her mouth into his, she took charge until he dominated her again. The kiss was rough and beautiful. It was like a tornado, wiping out everything that stood between them.

She straddled him, leading him as he lay on his back against the bed. Sensations ran up her body as his fingers slid between her thighs. She ached there from his touch before, but she wanted more. The blood roared through her body, thundering between her ears. Toni curled her fingers under the elastic of his boxer briefs and pulled urgently as he lifted his hips. She held her breath until his erection sprang out with such force, his cock smacked against his stomach. Wrapping her hand around the thick girth, she gasped. Holy shit, he would destroy her with it. He could literally destroy her in every way a person could be destroyed.

"Oh, Fabian..." Her voice was weak as she held his stone-like flesh in her hands. "I... I..."

He wrapped a hand around hers. She shifted her gaze up to meet his.

"I'm going to worship every part of you until you can't take me anymore. And then I'll stop and wait until you want me again."

Oh God. She wanted him inside her, filling her,

and didn't care if he made her walk crooked for a week. She's take every inch of him. "I want you inside, Fabian. So deep inside me you get caught."

She lifted herself to her knees and hovered over his incredible erection, biting her lip with anticipation of its entry. He stroked himself slow and languid before rubbing his tip against her. He paused, she groaned. "Condom in my wallet."

Of course. She'd been so lost in her wanton need, she'd forgotten that important thing.

Anticipation moved her into action. She retrieved the condom from his wallet and opened it with a sloppy tear. "Let me," she insisted, rolling the latex over his length, though there wasn't enough to cover him fully. Toni stared at him, sheathed and ready to penetrate her. She'd never describe a penis as beautiful, but his was. Perfectly shaped and angled. How would it feel? She gulped, taking a longer look at him.

"I won't hurt you, baby. I promise. I'll go slow." He soothed her fear. "Do you trust me?"

A week ago, the answer would have been a resounding no. Now, she couldn't imagine not trusting him. With everything.

She nodded. There was nothing else to say, only act on their shared desire. To quench the hunger that had been building since he became her assistant. It seemed so long ago, mere weeks, but time was arbitrary for her.

He took her hips in a firm grip, placed her over him just barely above his sheathed erection and whispered, "It won't be the same anymore after this."

With her own desperate whisper, she managed to say, "I don't want it to be the same."

Before she could take another breath, he was inside her, stretching her, impaling her. Her cried echoed in the room, as she tossed her head back, the pain much worse than what she thought it would be. It was as if she'd never been with a man before. Waves of pleasure came fast and furious as he slid further inside her. To the hilt, she took him in, holding still for a moment to let her body adjust to his size. She rose steadily, moaning with how much satisfaction came after.

"Ah … you feel so good. I can't…You're amazing." He choked on his words.

She lowered herself and lifted again, riding him at her own pace. He groaned, taking her waist and flipping her on her back. She yelped with the surprise.

He kissed her again with hot wet lips. His tongue infiltrated her mouth, meeting her tongue and tangled with it in a slow dance. The kiss was sensual, lasting for minutes. He parted from her, his voice gruff against her ear. "I was going to come fast if you stayed on top."

She lifted her hip against him. "You can. I want you to."

"No," he said, taking her buttocks in his hands. "I'm still working on you."

She squeezed around him, loving that he was still inside her. She throbbed, groaning as he plunged inside her harder this time. Several times he did that, finding his rhythm. Though they were having sex, she knew it was more than that. Despite how rough he was, how dominant he was, his eyes contrasted what their bodies did. They were making love. Nothing would convince her otherwise.

Time hung still between them as they continued to move together. Tension slowly built until they both released in a fierce explosion. After the high wore down, their eyes met. No, nothing would be the same between them.

Chapter Eighteen

The society pages would have a field day with this fact—Fabian Pallis had fallen hard. It was disconcerting, yet the most exciting thing he'd ever felt. He had *fallen*. It was worth saying again. Finally, someone made him fall. And that someone had called him a loose cannon and a misogynist. He lay with Toni, stroking her loose waves as he thought of the events that brought them together in his bed. Ten orgasms later. Six for her and four for him, and he wouldn't have it any other way.

"You probably should have fired me."

"I know." She moaned softly against his cheek.

He laughed. His smile faded until his face was resting against the pillow. Toni shifted under him, nuzzling him a moment before her mouth pulled in a weary smile. He brought his fingers to her lips, moving across them in a slow stroke. "I love these lips. I want them on me all the time."

She kissed his fingertips, taking them between her lips. God, she felt so good biting him like that. She pulled back, resting her head on the pillow next to him. "I never thought this would happen."

Fabian pulled her back to him, didn't want her a centimeter away from him. Not now. Not anymore. "I wanted this to happen the first second I saw you."

"I know you're probably still pissed at me for lying to your dad." She sighed, looking away. But when she looked back, her eyes were filled with so much, and he didn't know how he could ever possibly be mad at her about anything.

"Why didn't you just talk to me about it?" He recalled the email, not feeling any of the anger he once did. Actually, it made sense.

She shrugged. "I guess I was just fighting it. Fighting what I felt for you. It was really stupid."

"It's really sweet."

She smiled back at him. "I want you there as long as I can keep you. And I lied." The smile faded as she looked off for a moment, recounting something.

"Hey…" He stroked her face. "My father and I have bigger beef than you calling me a misogynist."

"But it's ruined your chances to join sooner, right?"

"Yeah." He nodded.

"I tried to talk to your dad at the gala. I'll talk to him now." She turned, attempting to get off the bed. But he wouldn't allow it. He grabbed her and pulled her back to the sheets they'd warmed.

"Let him think it. For now." He kissed her. "I want to keep you in my bed as long as I can."

A smile parted her lips. "How can this work?"

Her skin sprouted goose bumps as he ran his fingers over her collarbone and then back against her neck. "We'll make it work. Fuck what anyone else thinks. I don't give a shit. I just want you, Toni. And I know you feel the same way now."

"What about Camille? Is she in the picture?" She didn't look at him.

"No!" His emphatic response jolted her gaze up. In her eyes, he saw the uncertainty that he wanted to quell. "She's never been in the picture. Not like this." Reaching out, he trailed a finger over her skin, moving up her arm. He would never be able to stop touching her skin.

She sat up, the sheet slipping, exposing a nipple he promptly touched, because, well, he rather loved her nipples. She giggled like she was shy and pulled up the sheet again. She grew serious. "This has to be between us."

"What?" His stomach rippled. Was Stephan in the picture after all? "Why?" No way was he going to keep her a secret. He wanted the world to know she was his.

Toni touched his shoulder, hanging onto it. "It's … it's complicated. As long as you're working for me, we can't tell anyone."

Fabian watched her. There was more to this than she was letting on. Still, he could understand her point. Apparently, they'd been warned of each other. He also didn't want to jeopardize his chances of being partner with his dad. But he had to make sure another person wasn't the reason she wanted to keep their relationship a secret. "Is it Stephan?"

"No." Her gaze fell, and he worried. "I have no intentions of ever being with him. I want you."

"I want you too, baby. I don't want to hide this." His pulse beat wildly at his throat.

He knew she was troubled by the way she avoided eye contact with him. "Fabian, please see my point of view."

He wanted to soothe her, take the worried look off her face. The subject would be dropped. For now. He pulled her against him, felt the warm tresses of her silky hair on his chest. "Okay, baby. We can keep it between us. But for now." He backed away, lifting her chin with his finger. "But just until I leave RI. After RI, I intend for everyone to know you're with me. Understand?"

She fell against him. His arms tightened around her as if he'd never let go. And he wouldn't. *How did I get so fucking lucky?*

"You looked absolutely stunning in that dress tonight. Every man in the room wanted you." He recalled the way his father did, too, by the salacious look on his face. Disgusting. Competing for women was not a problem he and his father ever had, thank God.

"I only had eyes for you." Soft kisses tickled his chest. One by one, she moved up until her lips met his. They kissed soft at first, then more savage as his body warmed up again. Sweet and wet, her mouth opened and closed at his command when he'd taken control. And just like that, he put her down on her back and worked his way down with the intention to give her a seventh orgasm.

* * * *

Toni padded against the tiles in Fabian's kitchen, wobbling about like she'd been on a horse for twelve hours straight. With his size, she felt like she had been.

"I miss you," Fabian called from the living room. She'd braved the walk to the kitchen to fetch another bottle of wine to complement the Thai takeout.

She smiled. Not what she expected him to say? Wasn't he supposed to be a player? He'd been anything but since he found her on his doorstep. She laughed, calling out, "I'll be back in two seconds!"

He popped his head in the kitchen. "Two seconds is too long, my ladycakes."

Toni attempted to pull the cork from the bottle. "Well, well. The player has a ladycake."

Warm arms circled her from behind. She wore one of his t-shirts that was large enough to be a dress on her. He nuzzled her ear. "I guess the player was waiting for your cakes specifically."

How many ladies were there? She hated that thought, and didn't really want to know. But she'd only been with one other person, so the concept of casual sex was foreign to her. "Because my cakes are tasty."

"Mm. Indeed." He kissed her neck, and goose bumps sprouted all over her body. God, he felt so good.

She didn't want him to ever take his hands off her.

She moaned. Too distracted to continue the uncorking, her fingers slipped. "I can't believe it's past nine. I should probably go home. I don't have any clothes."

"We have a carton of pad Thai to eat. Besides, I like you in my shirt."

"I can't wear your shirt forever!" She laughed, turning to him. He was so cute standing there looking at her. Damn playboy. But his eyes were different, softer. He'd never looked as innocent as he did staring at her right then.

"Then I'll buy you a whole new wardrobe to keep here."

"Fabian, I have a wardrobe."

"Yeah, but I was thinking playsuits and teddies. Of the lace variety, obviously."

Toni slapped his arm. "You're a perv, aren't you?"

His eyes darkened. The breath caught in her throat when he said, "I'm a lot of things with you."

They kissed again for the millionth time. Tender and long, each of his kisses always felt like the first. The ground fell out beneath her—she was falling. Worries of her mother, of Stephan, of her need to prove herself couldn't touch her in that place with Fabian. He was all she needed. And so she kissed him harder. His hands slipped under the too-large shirt, driving up her ribcage until he cupped her breasts. She moaned. His hands were so gentle on her. He was so gentle. Not what she thought he'd be.

After they'd made love again on the counter of his kitchen, they sat on the floor taking turns drinking wine straight from the bottle. Her mother would freak if she knew where her daughter had ended up. Toni stared at her naked legs stretched out before her against the cool tiles. She thought of Stephan. How would she explain his presence at RI? She looked at Fabian's admiring gaze. He smiled, and she knew she wouldn't be able to tell him about Stephan. About what her mother wanted. The engagement.

How would she ever get out of that and still keep Fabian?

"Tomorrow's Monday."

"Mm-hmm." Fabian gulped from the bottle.

"Tomorrow is my month anniversary as acting CEO." Hard to believe the weeks had passed so quickly. She'd been whipped up by the events. Honestly, she hadn't been able to breathe.

"We need to celebrate." He handed her the bottle, which she promptly took a long swig.

"We can't celebrate if this relationship is supposed to be secret." Fabian frowned, and she quickly added, "For now."

"For exactly how long?" His stare pinned her. She couldn't look away even if she tried.

The answer didn't come. Because she had no idea, though what popped in her head was horrible. Unfathomable. *For as long as my mother is living*. She looked away in shame. There had to be a way. *Had* to. "Hopefully not long."

Chapter Nineteen

Fabian's heart fluttered upon his entry into Toni's office. He felt like a damn schoolgirl crushing on the hot, young English teacher. He carried a cup of Toni's special coffee and a file of investments he'd conned from the investment department's administrative assistant. He didn't knock before he opened the door—didn't think he had to anymore. She promptly looked up from her computer.

Her gaze impaled him. Her mouth opened from the surprise, making him hard thinking of what they did for most of Sunday. And just two hours ago in her penthouse.

"Hi beautiful," he said, kicking the door closed.

Her smile widened. She was the most beautiful woman he'd ever seen. Never did he think he'd be obsessed with someone like he was with Antonia.

"Hi." Her voice was low, seductive, making him silent promises.

"God, I miss your lips." Upon his approach, she stood. They kissed. He knew her perfect pink lipstick was ruined. It became his mission to ruin her lipstick every chance he got.

When they parted, she nervously glanced at the door. "Fabian, we have to be careful."

He groaned against her lips. "You know I can't *not* touch you if you're close to me." His fingers trailed up her bar arms. "I'm so hard right now."

She whimpered, their lips touching again. "No," she whispered, pushing him away. "We can't. I don't want anyone to walk in and see us."

Only one person came to mind. Stephan. "Why is that asshole here?"

173

She looked away. "It's my mother's doing. She wants him here." She took her coffee cup, drinking from it. "I don't want him here either. Trust me." Her eyes refused to meet his. What was she not telling him? The thought niggled at him. But, given their fresh relationship, he didn't want to pull at that string. Not yet.

He raked his hand through his hair. "I don't like it. And I don't want you having dinner with him. I still can't believe you did that after when happened at the bar."

"I promise I only went because my mother set it up. She wants us to … make nice." She looked away and he was sure she was keeping something from him. "I think she wants him to take over as CEO. Officially."

What? He paused, replaying her words. When he confirmed to himself that he'd heard right, he asked, "Are you kidding me?" He could barely find the voice to protest. "Why didn't you tell me this before?"

"Because it didn't matter before." She walked to the window. The distance grew between them, and he hated it. Finally, she turned to him. "If I have to go to dinner with him, it's just for show, Fabian. Just until we can announce we are together."

He stormed toward her, slowing when her eyes widened. Sometimes his passion got the best of him. Greek genes, he surmised. "Where is Helene in all this? Why is she putting all this on you if she has no intention of appointing you CEO?" He'd love to have a few words with the infamous Mrs. Robuchon.

"Please, Fabian. Don't ask me any questions right now. I'm trying to figure out how we're going to work."

With her words, he took her in his arms, calming the anger that bubbled up at the new information. How could he be the cause of more strife? He simply couldn't. But would wait until she could give him the answers he needed. "Okay … okay." The harder she trembled, the tighter he held her. "I'll deal with it."

"Thank you." Her words were muffled in his chest.

"But I can't for too long. You're with me. I'm not going to hide it." No response hurt his ego. He needed the validation that what they had was real and would survive whatever Toni was dealing with. He wished she'd trust him with whatever ailed her. But he relented, calming the rapid beat of his heart before he changed the subject. "I have something for you." He let her go, walked to the desk where he'd dropped the manila folder and opened it. Inside were three new investments he'd *acquired.* Unofficially, of course. "I charmed the investments admin to give me a look at new proposals."

"She gave that to you before the execs?"

"I'm good with women." He let his Pallis side smile emerge. Toni didn't seem quite as annoyed that time to receive it.

"Player." She laughed as she took a page in her hand. "Another biotech company."

"I only took the biotech ones." He picked up the second page in the folder. "This one is for a nerve sheath that protects the Vagus nerve during electro-stim therapy. They have FDA and EU approvals but now need capital for manufacturing. I did a quick read on user needs for this type of product, and I think this can be a good investment in conjunction with NeuRx and other neurostimulation companies we might invest in."

"Wow. *You* should be an exec." She continued to scan the pages. Finally, she looked up. "You're brilliant."

His heart thumped as he put the page back in the folder. "Nah. I just understand bioengineering."

"Yeah, and obviously you're the only one in this company that does." She shook her head. "How can we get the execs to approve NeuRx? How can we get them to hear me out? Hear us out?"

The smile came effortlessly. "Us?"

"Well, yeah." She dropped the page on the desk. "I couldn't do this without you."

"You could." Fabian caressed her cheek because it was the only thing he wanted to do when she was looking at him that way. All the uncertainty he knew she felt about herself showed through her eyes. "And you will."

Fabian dipped his head to kiss her just as the door flew open. They both turned to face the interruption. Stephan. He glared at them as he advanced into the office.

"What's going on in here?" he directed to Toni, another sharp glance to Fabian.

Heat rose through Fabian's body.

"We're discussing work." She sat in her chair. "What do you want?"

"I want to go over the NeuRx proposal."

Fabian's ears perked up. A bad feeling came over him. Stephan had no reason to ask for the denied proposal … unless he was thinking of claiming the updates as his own.

"My proposal?" Toni didn't hide her panic but recovered quickly.

"Your proposals are property of RI." Stephan smirked. "I read it over the weekend."

"How the hell did you get it?" Fabian chimed in, his voice deep and booming. Stephan obviously acquired it without Toni's knowledge.

"You don't have a muzzle for your assistant, Antonia?" He didn't dare look at Fabian. *Ass*. Fabian grew hotter, knowing he needed to leave immediately if he wanted to stay out of trouble—and jail.

"That's enough, Mr. Pallis." She turned to him, all too aware of Stephan. Her eyes widened. "You may leave now."

Stunned. He was literally stunned and hurt with her words. But he quickly reminded himself it was just for show. He nodded, not bothering to acknowledge Stephan. "Of course. I'll be in my office if you need me."

Just before he turned the knob to his office, Toni called to him. "Mr. Pallis…" He turned to meet her gaze, something shining in them gave him hope. "Before you go to lunch, come see me. I need to … show you something."

He smiled. He indeed knew what that meant.

* * * *

"I don't like him in here."

"He's my assistant, for God's sake, Stephan." And he was so much more. Keeping that secret would probably kill her. But the more she looked at Stephan, remembering her duty to her mother, the more she thought her and Fabian's secret may never see the light of day.

"He needs to be in a cube with the other secretaries." His darkened eyes shifted to Fabian's office door. He approached her, leading with a frown. "Where were you the rest of the weekend? I haven't seen or heard from you since the gala."

Having incredible sex. If only she could say that to his face. "I was busy."

"I need you to be available to me at all times, Antonia. We are a couple now," he chastised her, and she was really getting tired of other people deciding her relationship status.

"No, we are not a couple," she barked with some restraint.

He cocked his lip up into a smirk. "T.B.D., love."

Toni ignored him, and his stupid smirk. She needed him out. "Why do you want to talk about my proposal?"

"I'm going to have a meeting about it with the execs. I read the technology breakdown, and I think it was wrongfully passed up."

Her stomach flopped. "You are not going to talk to them about it. It's *my* proposal. Fabian completed that technology breakdown."

"Ah, so he's good for something after all then."

"You bastard!" Indignant, Toni stood and pages from the new investments went flying about. She snatched the raining pages as quick as she could.

"The meeting is set for Thursday afternoon. You can come if you want. It makes no difference to me." He winked and pivoted on his expensive heels toward the door. "Oh, and by the way, I'm taking you to dinner tonight."

"I can't!" Toni's fists balled at her sides. "I have yoga."

Stephan didn't turn. "Cancel." Before she could protest, he was on the other side of the door, leaving her fuming.

By lunchtime, she had calmed down. A little. Not really, actually.

But her initial desire to jab a pen in Stephan's eye had passed. Sort of. She'd spent the better of three hours planning her next move with the executives. If Stephan passed the updated proposal as his, he would be a shoo-in with the team in terms of becoming the official CEO. Toni just couldn't let that happen.

"You alone?" Fabian poked his head into her office.

She smiled. One look at him and that's all she could do. Her heart soared when he was close to her, and the butterflies … the butterflies rippled her stomach. No one had made her that weak in the knees before. Not even Stephan when she was convinced she loved him back then. "Not anymore." She stood and walked over to him to kiss him. Afterward, she was breathless. Everything, all her worries, fell away.

"I could kill Stephan for talking to you like that."

She shook her head, leaning in. He smelled so good. "I just want to get out of here."

"I know of a place." Strong arms wrapped around her. "Clothes are optional."

Naked with Fabian was exactly where she wanted to be. She laughed. "Perfect."

He kissed her again, their lips opening the moment they touched. When he broke the kiss, he was breathless. "I need you in my bed. Now." He cupped her ass, pressing her against his erection. She moaned with wanting him as much as she did.

Two hours later, Toni lay in Fabian's bed, satisfied and more relaxed than she'd ever been. "You're going to wear me out." She turned on her back.

"I'm not even finished, baby." He rolled on his side, a smile on his face.

She studied him. His eyes. His skin. His thick hair messed up from their tryst. Nothing about the way he looked at her ever suggested he was once a player. She always wanted to see him look at her that way. His lips curled up. He had no idea how lovely he looked. Not gorgeous. Or hot. Or all the things women would describe his as. Just lovely.

"What?"

Toni shook her head, a sudden knot of emotion balling in her throat. "Just … you."

Fabian didn't respond. Not with words. He lifted himself, moving down her body until he was between her legs, kissing her hipbones and running soft fingers over her sex. She moaned as his tongue trailed down and found her clitoris, bulging with the sudden thump of desire. Out of pure wanting, her legs opened further, allowing him access. Nothing would get in their way. He licked her slow at first, awakening her sensations once again. She was sure they'd been drained temporarily, but more came, growing in intensity with each lap on her sensitive skin. She nearly burst from wanting him.

She cried out, "Fabian!"

He moaned against her. Vibrations of his voice shot through her, making her orgasm fiercer. First, she saw stars, and then his handsome face stared down at her. Fabian's mouth was on hers again. Three hours after they'd arrived at Fabian's "sweet pad", or "love pad", as he'd referred to it in the car on the way there, they had been lying together, reveling in their love-making.

"I don't want to go back." Toni held him close, his raw masculine scent all over her.

"Let's ditch the rest of the day."

"Oh, God." She sat up, completely aware of time and space, which she'd temporarily had no clue of with Fabian. Her work dilemma came back to her. She'd need to force the executives to meet with her somehow.

"What?" He also sat up.

"Stephan is going to talk to the execs about our proposal on Thursday. He's going to pass off the technology breakdown as his own." She was frantic.

"What?" Fabian roared, his whole body tensed. "That son of a bitch."

"I can't seem to get a meeting with all of them before Thursday." She bit her bottom lip. "I don't know what to do."

"Talk to your mother." It was a demand.

She shook her head. That was a lost cause. "I've

tried to talk to her. She agrees with the execs."

"But if we show her…"

Toni's stomach twisted. All the pleasure she'd felt only moments ago was gone. She was left with the anxiety of her reality. "She won't hear me out, Fabian. I've tried. Trust me."

His jaw clenched. "There has to be something we can do to stop it."

She wanted to believe it. With her whole self she did. Pushing the sheets off her legs, she stood from the bed. "We should go back."

He nodded, deep in thought. "I hope I don't see that bastard."

"I hope I don't either." But she would, though. At dinner that night. And she wasn't going to mention it. Not then, anyway.

Chapter Twenty

Fabian sat in his office at half past six, staring at his email inbox. Something needed to be done about Stephan and his intention to hijack the NeuRx proposal and claim the update as his own. The thought sickened Fabian.

"Hi." Toni poked her head in the office. She looked surprisingly relaxed. Like she had after he'd made her come three times that afternoon. It was a good afternoon. He would gladly do it again had they not been in the office. It had been after hours, though...

"Hi, baby—I mean Miss Robuchon." He chuckled.

Her eyes grew wide. "Fabian. I told you about that." She glanced behind her and turned back with her beautiful smile that made his knees weak. She grew serious then. "Listen ... I have to have dinner with Stephan tonight."

Fabian scarcely contained his anger at the information. "Excuse me?"

"Please, Fabian. We talked about this." She walked into his office, closing the door behind her.

Anger gripped him so tight he couldn't look at her. To think of his girl with Stephan made him insane. A crazy person at best. "I hate this." *One. Two. Three.* He counted his heartbeats until he didn't want to punch something. Fabian looked up at her, his guilt taking over at the distress on her face, sagging the edges of her eyes. He knew he was wrong. It was temporary, he had to remind himself. Again. "Okay ... I know. I'm sorry. I just hate that you have to be around him after everything he did. And continues to do."

"It's just temporary," she said again, striding over

to him. He nodded, and could only accept the kiss she planted on his lips. Just then a voice called from her office. She backed off instantly. "Oh, shit."

Stephan opened the door. "Chop-chop, Antonia."

"So just file the rest of the correspondence before you leave. Okay?" Her voice wavered, and since her back was to Stephan, Fabian could see the desperation in her eyes.

"Anything you say, boss." It was best he looked at his computer screen while Stephan took his girlfriend away.

The silence after the click of the doorknob only increased the rage growing inside him. Without further contemplation, he placed his fingertips on the keyboard and typed like the wind.

To: Helene Robuchon(h.robuchon@robuchoninvestments.biz)

From: Fabian Pallis(f.pallis@robuchoninvestments.biz)

Date: Monday, July 25

RE: Important Information on NeuRx Proposal

Attachment: NeuRxUpdatedbyToni.doc

Dear Helene –

I have not been able to thank you for my employment, and I would like to take this opportunity to do so. Working with your daughter, Antonia, and with the Robuchon Investment staff has given me a foundation for working in a professional environment, which I plan to take to Pallis Engineering. That being said, I would like to discuss something critical. Antonia has re-proposed an investment deal with the NeuRx startup. The initial white paper written by RI didn't break down the technology in an effective way. As I am a bioengineer per formal education, I looked over Antonia's proposal and included more information that I believe should be considered and accepted by the executive team. This proposal is Antonia's alone, and she should retain full credit. Please see the attached document with complete technology breakdown. If you have any questions regarding the technology, please don't hesitate to ask. I hope you are well and look forward to your response.

Sincerely,
Fabian Pallis
CEO Executive Assistant
Robuchon Investments

If they couldn't stop Stephan's meeting, Helene was going to know whose idea Stephan was stealing. Fabian read the email twice, and with one press of his finger, the email shot off into cyberspace forever.

* * * *

Toni rubbed her hands together, taking in the full sight of her mother on the cushioned lounge chaise perched nearly over the crisp blue swimming pool in her River Oaks backyard. The two-acre backyard was a good size for the neighborhood.

"Are you too cold?" It was evening—after eight—and not cool at all. In fact, it was still ninety degrees. Toni had cut dinner short to speak to her mother. She gazed at her mother with debilitating sadness as she lay on the lounge chair, wrapped in a light gauze throw.

Her mother waved her hand away. "I won't get to see this much longer."

Toni's stomach rippled, vomit bubbling up inside her. She might actually hurl herself into the pool. So much to say to her mother, so little time. So little strength to actually pull it off. "I've really enjoyed working at RI the last month. I feel like I could make it permanent."

Though her large framed sunglasses hid her eyes, Toni knew her mother's intense gaze pierced her. "Now, why on earth would you want to do that?"

"Well, I do have an MBA from Rice, Mother."

An odd smile pulled at her mother's thin skin. "Yes, darling. All the women in this family have an advanced degree. You know my MBA is from Harvard."

"Where you met Daddy." It was a pinch to Toni's heart, reminding her what a lovely man her father was. God, she missed him.

"Yes. Just like you met Stephan at Rice." The smile faded, followed by a cough.

Toni's gaze dropped again to her thighs against the lounge chair. Dread and all those shitty feelings took up residence inside her. How in the living hell was she supposed to broach the subject of being CEO to her mother? Not to mention the fact that she was with Fabian, *not* Stephan. But she was a grown woman now, not the little girl who was told when to sit and cross her legs and when to sip her tea. *Screw this.*

"Mom ... I want to be CEO." There, she said it with a wavering voice maybe, but it was out there. Words to the ears that needed to hear it.

From under the sunglasses, her mother's arched eyebrow lifted. The pool lighting gave her an otherworldly effect. She didn't say anything for ages, which made Toni feel she hadn't heard her. She even considered saying it again, but her mother finally spoke.

"Stephan is my choice to run RI after I'm gone, Antonia. I've already told you this."

It was now or never. "What about me, Mom? Did I go to Rice for nothing?" Her throat ached with the words that came out. Finally. Tears came out too. As she stared at the reflection of her mother's sunglasses, Toni felt guilty about challenging her mother's last wish. How cruel of a daughter was she?

Her mother remained calm as ever. "Not for nothing, silly girl. For legacy. The women in the

Robuchon family are well educated. Look at Grandmother Robuchon. She was a medical doctor, educated at Oxford. Didn't practice a day in her life." She shook her head, the scarf wrapped around her head waved with the motion. "You knew what you'd be, darling, and that is married to a Bradley. The most powerful family in Houston. I dare to say Texas. It's been an agreement for a long time."

"Mr. Pallis is powerful too." Toni hoped she didn't reveal too much. Maybe that was exactly what she wanted to do, though.

Her mother's left brow lifted again. "Are you speaking of big Pallis or little Pallis?"

Toni could barely meet her mother's stare now that she'd taken off her sunglasses. Even the threat of imminent death couldn't soften the edge in her eyes. In a broken, tortured voice—much like her poor heart beating wildly in her chest—she confessed, "I don't want to marry Stephan."

Her mother grunted, followed by a violent spell of coughing that sent her medical aid, Ms. Keller, into action. Toni's mother waved her away with a sharp swipe. "You can leave me, Ms. Keller. I'm managing." She coughed again. "Stephan is perfect, and you could do worse. Obviously, you have, but I won't let you."

"Mom—" Toni stood, ready to corral her mother if she kept coughing like that. The sight made her feel ill.

"No." It was a harsh one syllable word. Toni glanced to the nurse who reluctantly nodded and left the poolside. "Sit down, Antonia. This death is playing with me. Your father must be having a good laugh up there."

"Mom, please…" She couldn't manage much after that.

"I want to see him, you know. I want this to be over so I can see him again. Is it so hard to have my one last wish, Antonia?"

Toni sucked in her stomach. She knew what her mother meant. Every word. She'd struggled with it since before Fabian had come into her life. Toni shifted her blurry gaze to her fingers woven together in her lap.

"Oh, don't look like that. Like a whipped dog. That has always been your problem."

The words cut her, deep and painful. Her mother shredded her. Is that what she thought of her daughter? A whipped dog? Toni wanted to shout. To defy her mother.

"Leave now. I need to rest." Toni stood slow and steady, so many words at the brim of her lips desperate to spill out. Her mother added, "I hope you can sort out your situation before Stephan proposes, which will be soon, I suspect."

"What?" Her body stilled. *Oh, God, no!*

"And fire Pallis. He needs to move on." She turned from Toni, calling to her nurse.

"But it's only been two weeks." Toni shut her eyes, caught between anger and debilitating sorrow. How could she face Fabian after this? How would she tell him?

"He's done enough damage."

Chapter Twenty-One

Tuesday morning came around with no response from Toni the night before. Fabian had texted her, anxious to know what happened at her dinner—her forced dinner. He'd never felt so out of control in his life. It was killing him slowly.

He arrived at Toni's penthouse, grateful that concierge had let him up without any problems. "Thanks, man," he said, striding to the elevator banks with too much energy fueling him. Everything around him played out in slow motion, yet also fast forward. He didn't have a good feeling about anything anymore. All the way up to the top floor, his thoughts shot forth in all directions. When he finally stood in front of her door, his mind went blank.

Toni opened the door after a few knocks. Her eyes looked different, distant. Fabian reached for her, hugging her though not getting back the same intensity. Something was wrong. "Baby?"

She pulled away from him, walking quickly into the living room with him on her heels. Still in her robe, she paced and when she was near him again, she said, "What do we really know about each other? We're practically strangers."

His heart dropped to his stomach. Shaking his head, he said, "We aren't."

She turned away from him again. "We are. You don't know three things about me."

A second hadn't passed before he was behind her, heat rising up his face as he spoke. "Oh, I don't? Really?" She turned to face him, her eyes blazing. He continued on pure adrenaline alone because he couldn't handle her running away from him anymore. He was ready to fight.

"I know you're afraid of yourself."

"What?" Her eyes betrayed her. He nailed it and she knew it. "That's just stupid. I'm not afraid of myself."

"You're not?" He pointed at her. Clearly, she wasn't a fan of it as she swatted his finger away. "You've been told who you're supposed to be since birth and you don't trust yourself to be who you really are. That's why you're basically a mini-Helene, commanding and demanding. You don't even like to do it, I see through that act. And I know you can't possibly be so goddamn particular about your coffee. Give me a break! One cup of organic skim milk and a tablespoon of cane sugar? Get the hell out of here with that bullshit!"

"Don't put your finger in my face!" She slapped his hand again, that time a low *smack* reverberated through the air. The woman could swing. The sting of her skin stayed on his hand a few seconds longer. She turned away. Fabian wasn't sure if she needed to take a breath or cry. Her expression implied she might do both, and he felt the exact same way. He advanced to her, but as much as he wanted to take her, hold her, he didn't. She probably wouldn't let him anyway.

She turned to face him again, unwavering determination set in her dark eyes. "And you're really one to talk about trusting yourself."

His jaw clenched. It was war now. "What the hell are you talking about? I trust myself just fine. I'm not the one running away."

She scoffed, crossing her arms over her chest. Little did she know her nipple poked out from under her arm. If he wasn't so pissed, he'd have paid more attention to it. Her words practically lunged at him, though. "Yeah, whatever, trust fund brat!"

Her words punched him in the gut. All the air

squeezed out of him. His vision blurred the microseconds he let that statement destroy him. "What did you call me?"

In that moment, she was reflecting the worse of himself. They both knew it. "You heard me, Pallis. If you trusted yourself at all, you wouldn't be living off your trust fund with no direction in your life. I mean, let's be honest, are you really going to be a partner at your dad's firm?"

He was stunned, shot in the heart. He might want to vomit a little, but that wasn't a manly thing to do. Fabian gathered his thoughts. They oscillated between agony and sheer anger. Not toward Toni, but toward himself. With all this spinning through his mind, he only managed, "I will be."

"*Right*." God, she was so smug with that one word. A word he normally liked. Not that time.

He decided to bring out a bigger gun. "So why are you acting CEO, then? Oh, right, because you're one big phony actress! You told me yourself you want to be the actual CEO, but you're too chicken-shit to go for it on your terms because you don't believe in yourself. If you actually believed you had anything to offer, you wouldn't let your mother or Stephan dictate your life like some goddamn puppet-master. Or take your ideas. If you believed in yourself at all, you would demand respect from those execs who treat you like shit. I know you're just as smart as they are, but you're too afraid to see that you have what it takes. You're afraid to fail. To be the bad daughter. The bad fiancée. To be *you*, damn it!"

Now it was her turn to look like she'd been hit by a bus. Tear-filled eyes turned up to him, wide with the pain she felt. They stared for a long time, too long, without any words. They didn't need words. Finally, she shook her head. "You might think you're strong because you won't let a woman into your heart. But that's weak."

The air caught in his throat. He reached for her. "I have, Toni. You." She pulled from him. "I'm not weak. I'm showing you I'm not. Isn't that enough?"

"No."

The words wouldn't come. They were like sounds whirling in his mind that he couldn't string together. "I don't understand what's happening here. What are you saying?"

She didn't touch him, only kneaded his insides with her stare. "It's over."

* * * *

He was right. Everything Fabian said to her was spot-on, and she didn't know how to reconcile her ability to continue the lie. She sat in the back of the Robuchon limo, Miles's gaze catching hers at times from the rearview mirror.

Damn it. Why did everything have to be so hard? She glanced down to her clenching fingers. She didn't want this life. But it was what her mother wanted, and how could she say no to her last parent? She'd do anything to have her father again…

"Miles, will you take me to Melina's?" Toni couldn't go to the office. She was too raw with emotion to face her acting gig. And Fabian.

His eyes met hers again. "Of course."

Toni pulled out her cell phone. She typed with fast fingers.

Toni: **Mel, are you home today? I need to talk ASAP.**

A response lit up the phone.

Mel: **OMG what's wrong? Come over.**

Toni: **OMW**

Twenty minutes later, Melina opened the door, dressed in a pair of dark denim pants and a fitted white blouse. "Toni?" Melina's gaze searched Toni's face. "Oh, honey, what happened?"

Toni shoved her way into the apartment, heading for the stash of vodka Melina kept in her freezer. Maybe it was only eight in the morning in Houston, but it was five in the evening somewhere else.

"Sorry," she said, once she'd poured herself a glassful.

"You're fine. Drink as much as you want." Melina leaned against the counter. "What happened?"

"I think I'm in love." The big gulp of vodka burned down each centimeter of her throat. Melina's eyes widened, but she didn't speak. Thank God. Toni hoped she wouldn't. "And it's with the wrong person." Well, to her mother it was the wrong person. To Toni, Fabian was the absolute right person.

Melina grabbed the bottle and took a swig nearly as large as the one Toni took. After each woman indulged in another swig, Melina spoke, a gleam in her brown eyes. "It's Fabian, isn't it?"

Toni fell against the counter, the hard edge catching her hipbone. "I'm so screwed."

"Why?" Melina's question proved she had no idea the kind of duty Toni had to her family. To society.

Toni knew she had to come clean about everything. Her mother. Her life. She didn't want to fool anyone anymore, especially not her best friend. "There is so much required to live my life. To wear those couture dresses … the price is high. And I don't want to pay anymore."

Melina's eyebrows creased. "What do you mean?"

"Mom wants me to marry Stephan."

She tried not to gasp. "You can just tell her you're in love with Fabian, can't you?"

Toni shook her head. If only it were that easy. "No. I can't. It's an agreement between the families."

"What?" Melina seemed appalled by the archaic concept.

"This world I live in is just one big business transaction. It's like a fucking corporation. I'm just a commodity." She cried then, the tears rushing down. Some dropped on her fingers gripping the glass nearly empty of vodka.

"I don't understand..."

It was time to say it out loud to someone else. Toni put the glass down and looked her friend square in the eyes. "My mom is dying. She has cancer."

Melina gasped, reaching for Toni again, though pulled back when Toni wouldn't allow her embrace. A broken whisper filled the space between them. "I'm so sorry."

Though she'd known for two months, the truth still left Toni paralyzed. Her mom was going to die, and it could be sooner rather than later. Her children would never know their grandparents. If she had any. Fabian came to mind in that very real and fleeting thought. She couldn't be sidetracked by all the things that would never happen. She sucked in a breath. "She's not going to last long, and that's why she appointed me to take her place at Robuchon Investments while she gets a *proper* CEO in place. A family member, by blood or marriage." The words killed her.

Melina's fingers flew to her mouth, her eyes shining with unshed. "I just don't know what to say."

Toni took the bottle, brought it to her lips and drank. Screw the glass. She stared down to her Valentino shoes, a cruel reminder. "She wants Stephan to be CEO." The words tasted as strong in her mouth as the ice cold vodka. But she felt sad after the truth came out, not numb like she'd hoped.

"Why not you?"

Toni wiped her cheeks again and again with her fingertips. "I'm not supposed to be a CEO. I'm supposed to be the trophy wife of a CEO."

Melina squinted—she didn't believe that shit.

Toni shook her head, and in a whisper confessed her desire. "But I want to be CEO. I want my mom to believe I can be the right CEO for RI. I know I can do it." She actually didn't until Fabian believed for her. He gave her the strength she needed to say what she wanted and believe it might be possible, even if something stood in the way. For that, she would always be grateful. And love him.

Melina took Toni in her arms, squeezing tight like it would be the last time they would embrace. Melina trembled as she held her friend. In a whisper, she said, "Tell her. Tell her it can be you."

"She's dying, Mel. I can't deny her. It's her last wish. How can I go against that? How can I?" She was feeling hysterical at that point, emotions rolling through her, making her dizzy—or maybe it was the vodka. Maybe it was the possibility that she would never have Fabian again. Worse was the reality that she would never have her own life.

Chapter Twenty-Two

Tuesday passed and not a word from Toni. She hadn't made it to the office, which Fabian wasn't totally surprised about. He wondered how he was able to make it in after she'd dumped him. Their relationship had barely started, and so quickly it was over. Over before it began. Something else was going on. It had to be. What else could change her heart so quickly? Up until that morning, he thought things were going well. He'd thought they were on the same page.

Maybe he was wrong. Obviously, he was.

That evening, Fabian kicked his feet up on the wooden bench at the La Grange patio bar, imbibing a Bloody Mary, trying to forget the look on Toni's face when she left him. Konrad was the only one who could give him an unbiased opinion. And not bust his chops for pure entertainment.

"Toni is a right bird, mate," Konrad interjected his thoughts. "I like her."

Taking another sip of Bloody Mary, he wished it was stronger. "This is weak piss. Why am I drinking this? It's not brunch."

Konrad signaled for the waitress who bounced over with a smile on her face. The women always were impressed with Konrad's sort-of British accent. Maybe they thought he was good-looking too, but it didn't matter. "Hey, love, can we get two more of these things. Strong. More Vodka. Chopin if you have it."

She nodded, holding his gaze a bit longer before Konrad looked away. "Of course."

"I think she likes you." Fabian shifted against the wooden seating. He sighed.

"You've got to make some sort of grand gesture,

mein frund." Konrad's eyebrows lifted a bit when he spoke in his native German. He'd learned to speak English in England, hence the sort-of British accent.

Fabian looked at his blinking phone. Notifications from social media had vibrated his phone all morning. Apparently, Camille thought she should share what she was felt about him on every social media site she was on. The last three days he'd avoided the internet for that reason alone. He raked a hand through his already sweaty hair. He would rather be in Cambridge during the summer than Houston. It was brutal, especially at five in the afternoon. Fabian took off his aviator sunglasses. "What's my reputation, Kon?"

"What do you mean?" Konrad acted like he didn't know, but he wasn't fooling anyone.

"You know what I mean." Fabian caught his friend's stare, wouldn't let go. He needed to hear the truth.

The waitress came back with two garnished drinks. Fabian's stomach rumbled. "Thanks, sweetheart."

"You're welcome." She smiled at Fabian, stalled a bit before she said more. "I heard about you and Camille."

Fabian sighed. That was old news. News he didn't want to be reminded of. News that was irrelevant now anyways. "Have we met?" He cringed. *Please let us have never met.*

A small laugh puffed from her lips. She shook her head, her gaze dropping to her fingers for a second. "No. But I just wanted to say … sorry. And if you want a drink anytime, come see me." She glanced at Konrad, who beamed like the big golden German boy he was. "You too, Konrad."

Once she left, Konrad commented before he took a large swig of his new drink. "And what was the question again?"

Fabian grunted. "Am I a useless prick?"

The defeatist in him reared his ugly head. That really wasn't the question he wanted to ask, though. No one else could answer the real question he had for himself. Which was—did he deserve Toni? And even though his first response was no, a deeper part of him said yes. He'd changed entirely too much since meeting her for the answer to *not* be yes.

"No, mate. You're a useless, feckless prick who shags women and doesn't remember them. But you've been that way since Harvard."

His skin burned. Stomach rumbled again. And he kind of wanted to punch his friend in the face. "So I should be a workaholic like you who doesn't know how to have fun?"

"I have fun. Making money is fun. And this isn't about me, Fabian. This is your shit, mate."

"*Ah, fuck.* I know." Fabian slipped his sunglasses back on his face, before sliding an open palm to the back of his neck. Damn, it grew hotter each second. He sat in the silence, trying to accept the thoughts that sprung forth. The awareness finally came after refusing to take a good look at himself after too many years.

Konrad spoke first. "Reputations can change, mate."

Fabian shook his head. "I never wanted anything. Not the money or the Harvard education. Or the good looks to get into as many panties as I have. Hell, I didn't even really want to be a partner in my dad's firm." He muttered, "I can't stand the bastard." Fabian put both elbows on table, letting the warm wood caress his skin. "But I want her. I ... I feel like I need her, man. I don't have the slightest clue how to handle myself. And today, when she ... my heart broke in half. I mean, physically.

Right in half, bro."

"Blimey! I think you might be in love." Konrad chuckled at first, then a string of laughter followed bordering on ridiculousness. "Fucking hell. I never thought that would happen. Cheers to that!" He lifted his Bloody Mary, and without Fabian following suit, clanked the air and tossed it back. Bacon and olives everywhere. "Shyte!"

"What do I do?"

"Phone her now. Tell her you want to see her."

Fabian hesitated. Was it really over between him and Toni? "But she broke up with me."

"Doesn't matter. People break up sometimes out of fear. Maybe something spooked her."

Energy surged through him. Konrad was right. The only thing that made sense was that she was afraid of something. With that in his mind, fueling him, Fabian scanned the place for a private area but decided a text might be better.

Fabian: **Toni, I'm going to call you tonight. Answer when I do. I need to talk to you.**

His stomach flopped the moment he pressed send. *Oh, God.* The rejection he could face—continued rejection. But there was an excitement inside him, thinking of all the things he wanted to say to her. All the things he wanted to do. A solid minute passed with no response. He set the phone on the table, watching it relentlessly for the rest of their conversation.

"I can't stand to think of Stephan there with her." He scrubbed his face. "She is way too good for him."

"That tosser Bradley. You know he'd been after me about investing in some real estate and I'm just not interested. It's a bad deal in my opinion." Konrad's gaze shifted to Fabian's phone. "Don't worry about him. He had his chance with her."

"I don't know what I'll do if she gives him another chance." He would die. Dead on the ground. "I would have to fight him, Kon. I might go to jail if she goes with him."

"Good thing your father has a good lawyer."

"No shit." He took another drink letting the possibilities sink in. Even created some scenarios in his head that had his heart beating double time. "I can't be without her."

Konrad looked stunned. Speechless at first, his blue eyes dilated with his thoughts—God only knows what they were. But Fabian might have had an idea.

"You're in deep, mate."

"I am."

* * * *

When Toni arrived at her penthouse it was after five in the evening. She'd spent the remainder of her day in Galveston, sitting inside the Robuchon limo, watching the tiny waves roll onto the sand. She didn't go outside. Miles didn't say a word the whole time, only waited for her direction. Miles was a good chauffeur.

She sat on her terrace looking over Montrose Boulevard, a flute of champagne between her fingers, because she hadn't had enough already in the limo. She'd counted two full bottles empty. Yet, she wasn't drunk. Not even a little bit, which was a shame because it was all she wanted. She read Fabian's text message at least a hundred times, not daring to respond. What would she say anyhow? It was over between them.

Five sips later, her phone vibrated from the glass top patio table. She jumped and snatched the phone up to read the screen. *Fabian.* She bit her lower lip, the pressure growing harder with each ring. If she bit it any harder, she'd break the skin for sure. It stopped. She sighed. The phone slipped between her fingers onto her lap. It was warm against her skin. Her insides were warm too.

An hour passed—two maybe—and she couldn't bring herself to listen to his voice message. Dueling desires played games with her head—and her heart. Fabian. Stephan. Her mother. Imagine if she'd said no to the life she was prescribed. Imagine what she would be in that moment … disowned by her only living parent. And surely, since she was an only child like both her parents, the end of the line for a family spanning generations of good connections and money. She had a duty to her family, what little there was left of it.

With trembling fingers, she lifted the phone from her lap. After taking one last lengthy glance at the sky, she began to tap on icons until she navigated to her email application. Reluctant for only a moment, she began to type.

To: Victor Pallis(Victor@PEngineering.biz)

From: Toni Robuchon(t.robuchon@robuchoninvestments.biz)

Date: Tuesday, July 27

RE:RE:RE: Fabian

Mr. Pallis – Per my mother, Helene Robuchon, I will release Fabian from employment tomorrow, Wednesday. There will soon be a change in management, and Fabian will no longer have a place. You should know that he has improved tremendously since my last report. I am positive he is ready to transition to your engineering firm as a partner. My mother and I are confident he is ready for the task. Fabian is unaware of my decision to release him. Please allow me to speak to him first. If you have any questions about my decision, please feel free to email or call me.

Sincerely,

Toni Robuchon
Acting CEO
Robuchon Investments

Chapter Twenty-Three

Fabian couldn't quite get the key inside the doorknob to his condo. On the fourth try, the door swung open, but it wasn't due to his own accord.

"What the hell are you doing, Fabian?" His father stood in front of him, a beer in his left hand and a sneer tugging at his lips.

"Dad." The shock sobered him a good amount. "What the hell are you doing in my condo?"

"Don't you mean *my* condo?" His father stepped aside to let Fabian stagger into the space. "You're drunk."

Fabian grunted, the haze lifting from his sight. "Well, not anymore, thanks to you." He turned to face his father standing by the closed door. "Just because you own this complex doesn't mean you own this condo."

"It sure as hell does, Fabian."

"I'll pay for it then."

His father's eyebrows lifted like thick furry crescents. "With what money?"

"With my money!" He was getting sick and tired of people suggesting he wasn't capable of earning a living, or anything else for that matter.

"Oh, your trust fund?"

Fabian's jaw clenched, but he contained the anger growing inside. Of all the nights to go off on his father, it seemed like a good one. But he was still too tender from the argument with Toni, he wouldn't be able to fight fair if he began. "I don't need the trust fund. I have plans that don't include you or your goddamn money."

"Well, according to this email, it's not money you'll be making at RI, that's for sure."

His heart skipped. "What are you talking about?"

Approaching at a threatening speed, his father

entered Fabian's personal space in no time flat. "Damn it, Fabian. What the hell are you doing with Helene's kid? And don't you lie to me." He waved his finger around. Fabian wasn't a fan.

"Get out of my face, Dad." He turned toward the floor-to-ceiling window stretching the length of the living room.

"Didn't I tell you she's off-limits?" The accusatory tone shook Fabian more than he expected. But his father wasn't done yet. "Someone saw you at the gala, Fabian. With Helene's daughter. There are rumors going around."

He turned in a flash. "What do you mean?" He knew exactly what it meant. Someone saw him kiss Toni. Saw him touch her. He closed his eyes, thinking of all the ways he touched her not that long ago. But there was something else he glossed over. "What email are you talking about?"

"Are you seeing Antonia behind my back?" His father's eyes darkened. When Fabian didn't answer, he asked again. Harsher that time. "Are you screwing Antonia, Fabian? After I told you to stay away from her?"

"Don't talk to me like that! And don't say her name like that either!" He had to be careful not to fall apart. Might be too late though, he was shaking harder than he ever had.

His father scrubbed his red cheeks. Fabian glanced behind his father, spotting the other beer bottles on the coffee table. "This is why you won't be partner at my firm. You don't listen. How can I trust you if you can't take a simple direction? Couldn't you keep it in your pants for once? Aren't there still a good number of girls you haven't screwed over yet since you got back from Cambridge?"

Gutted. That was the only way to describe how he felt. It had been the worst twenty-four hours of his life in a very, very long time. How easily his own father could say such things to him nearly killed him. Though he would have normally walked away from this fight, he was compelled to stay. His own hurt drove his words, and before the first one came out, he knew it would be the lowest point of his life after losing his mother.

"Like father, like son. I'm sure Mom would be so proud."

His father stopped as if he'd been hit by the Metro. He waved a bit too, must have been replaying the words to make sure he'd heard right. Fabian couldn't believe he'd actually had the nerve to say them. But he needed to. He'd always needed to, but it never seemed like the right time.

"Don't you dare. I cared about your mother." His father's voice dropped several octaves. Deep and a bit frightening, the voice took Fabian back to his childhood. But just for a second.

"You care about yourself. Don't ever say you cared about my mother. She would have stayed if you gave a damn about her." Fabian wanted to stop, but he couldn't. Adrenaline was pumping through him faster than he could censor his words. He braced himself for the blow he knew his father wanted to give him.

"You don't know anything about it, Fabian. Not a goddamn thing." The controlled tone sent a chill through Fabian's body. He'd never seen his father as contained as he had been in that moment. It was a new level of anger, and he was anxious of what would happen next. "If you ever mention your mother again like this, I swear I will cut you out of my will. Of my life."

"You cut me out a long time ago, Dad, when you stopped believing I could be something. If you ever believed it."

The anger drained from his father's body, his shoulders slumped over. A deflated expression followed. He reflected the agony Fabian felt inside. The thing that hung between father and son for so long needed to come out. Desperately. "I never cut you out, son. I hate that you think it."

In an instant, he was a tired man who looked all of his sixty years. Regret came fast, much like Fabian suspected it came for his father who transformed into the shell of a man standing before him. "Dad…"

He silenced Fabian with a slow lift of his hand. Fabian waited anxiously to meet his father's gaze. When he did, he saw his father for the first time. Completely raw and open. "I loved your mother, Fabian. I loved her like no other. But she wasn't from my world."

Fabian bowed his head, knowing this is what prompted her to abandon her husband and son, though he'd never heard his father say it. His mother was his grandfather's maid who his father inconveniently fell in love with.

"It was easier for her to hate me and leave on her own than to ask her to. I just could never do that."

Fabian's breath caught in his throat. "What?"

His father turned the opposite direction, running a thick hand over the top of his head. "Your grandfather wasn't a fan of me marrying the help. In fact, I was supposed to marry Helene. He never forgave me for giving her up to Robuchon. But Robuchon was a good man. Helene was better off with him."

Fabian couldn't speak if he tried. The words left him, and it was a whole minute until he understood his own thoughts. "Oh, shit." That was best he could do.

"Let's just say our circle isn't forgiving. Rich marry rich, that's just the way it goes. And when you don't, you aren't regarded the same. That's why I hope you'll sow your wild oats and marry Camille. She's new money, but everyone at some point is new money. It will be easier for your grandchildren."

"Why not Toni?" Why couldn't he stop carrying on like she was still an option? Because in his heart, he knew they weren't done.

"Helene would never allow that." He finally turned, his face etched with the hard truth. "We're still good friends, but I might as well be in exile for marrying your mother."

"But you said you loved Mom. How can that be bad?"

A slow grunt jerked his father's body. "There are a lot of things that should be good that are not, and a lot of things that should be bad that are not."

"But I want her, Dad. I want her so much I can't think straight." A spike of energy rushed through his body. Air lodged in his throat. A sense of doom fell over him. Fabian was about to get bad news by the look on his father's face.

"This is the only time I'll tell you to give something up. But you have to before it's too late."

"What do you mean? Give what up?"

"Antonia, son. She's going to let you go."

* * * *

"Toni, I need to talk to you. I need to make it right between us. I didn't mean what I said... Well, I did, but not the way it sounded. I don't care what it takes, I'll do it. I'll do whatever you want. I ... I think I'm in love with you. No. I know I am. Please call me."

Toni listened to Fabian's message a total of seventeen times. Over and over. "I think I'm in love with you" played on repeat in her mind. The sentiment was true for her as well. She was in all possible ways in love with him. But it was impossible.

She put her phone on the side table and turned over on her side promptly after. *Tomorrow is going to suck*. Hard. Her whole life would suck if she had to marry Stephan Bradley. *Ugh*. She flipped over on her back, the plush bed taking her in its depth. *Can a person stay in bed forever?*

Toni would have kept on her self-defeating pity party thoughts had she not heard a bang on the front door loud enough to penetrate a couple thousand square feet of space between her bed and the door. *What the hell?*

She bolted up and grabbed the velvet robe slung over the foot of her bed before rushing through her room, the long hallway, and the living room. The sound grew louder. A muffled cry of her name came from the other side. She knew who it was without looking through the peephole. And she didn't know the first thing to do.

"Fabian, what are you doing here?" She barely managed through her dry throat. She glanced at the clock on the opposite wall. "It's midnight! How did you get up here?" She'd have to have a serious conversation with the concierge.

"Open the door, Toni. Please open the door."

Tears sprung to her eyes from the sheer desperation in his voice—and the sheer desperation growing inside her. "I can't," she whispered.

"I know about the email." A thump followed his words. Toni imagined his forehead fell against the door. "Tell me why, Toni. Just tell me why."

She dropped her face against the door. Hard heartbeats sounded between her ears. Deep pulses reminded her she was very much alive. And he was very much on the other side of that door. Simply put, she wasn't ready to tell him why. *Damn Mr. Pallis*. She only needed one more night to dream until she had to let

Fabian go.

She opened the door fast. Might as well rip off the Band-Aid and do what she needed to do. Everything felt fast. Her eyes adjusting as he came into sight. Her breath sharply dragging in and out of her. Her blood rushing through her veins. Frantic and urgent, it was like a dream with a disorienting haze clouding him and her. But she needed to see him. She needed to fall in his arms as he stood there, broken and looking more gorgeous than he ever had. Her gaze dropped to his lips, the desire to kiss them came fast and hard. Her mouth watered with the hunger of it. In that moment, more than anything, she wanted to feel his lips on hers, opening slowly until their tongues met. Until he infiltrated her in all the ways she needed.

Instead, her words were slow to come. She croaked his name, a sigh reverberating through the space. "Fabian. Why did you come here? You shouldn't be here."

"Did you want me to wait until tomorrow for you to completely destroy me?" His green eyes blazed—neon irises contrasted a thick fringe of dark lashes.

"I'm destroyed too, Fabian," she cried, not stepping away from his advances toward her.

"Bullshit!"

She didn't pull away when he grabbed her wrists. "I am, damn it!"

"Why did I have to find out from my dad that you're going to fire me?"

"He wasn't supposed to tell you." She waved with his movements.

"Irrelevant, Toni." His fingers squeezed, eliciting a gasp from her. Bowing his head, he groaned. "God, I hate you so much right now, but all I want is to kiss you, goddamn it."

Tears stopped all the words from coming again. But she didn't want to say words to him, the man who was completely falling apart before her—because of her. Pure need catapulted her forward until her lips met his and they were locked in a kiss so passionate, her whole world flipped on its side. They kissed like savages starved for months. He reached around her waist, lowering until he cupped her buttocks and lifted her off her feet. She yelped, holding his shoulders. Somehow they ended up in her living room, the plush couch against her back.

"I want you, Toni," Fabian murmured against her mouth, palms riding up her sides to the elastic of her panties.

"I want to feel you," she whimpered at the prospect. She widened her legs to accommodate his size. One last time.

Fabian complied, pushing down his jeans, exposing his erection. She lifted her hips, allowing him to slide down her panties until they were skin to skin. He was so hard. Like the tortured look on his face. She was positive she looked tortured too.

In the next breath, he slid inside her, moving against her skin. So many sensations and no way to pinpoint how she felt. Need. Desperation. Full. Her whole body shuddered to take him as deep as she could, clenching so he couldn't separate from her. It was too hard to think this would be their last time. She pressed her lips against his, opening her mouth so he filled her in every way he could. God, she loved this man.

"I'm going to miss you," she whispered against his mouth.

"Hmm?" His eyes opened a brief moment. He didn't hear her, and for that she was half-glad.

"I'm going to come," she said louder, her voice

broken with the intensity of her looming orgasm. And she did. Harder than she'd ever experienced. Hard enough her eyes watered. "Fabian!"

Afterward, they lay against each other on the couch, both breathing heavy from their lovemaking. The silence spoke volumes—for each it was very different. When was she supposed to tell Fabian they couldn't be together? It was so cruel to do it then, but when wouldn't it be? She shifted under him.

He laughed. "We need a towel."

She sat up, his hand trailing down her back as she did so. "We need more than that."

"What do you mean?"

Shaking her head, she decided it was time. "We aren't back together, Fabian. This was just—"

"A goodbye fuck?" His response roared out of him, scaring her a bit. But when her eyes met his, she knew the pain he felt.

"There's too many things that are keeping us apart."

"Tell me one," he demanded.

She dropped her head in both hands, rubbing her skin until the urge to breakdown diluted. "I have responsibilities to my family. To my mom. I'm her only child."

"What does that mean?" He pulled her hands from her face. When she didn't answer, he touched her lips. "Tell me."

"My mom is sick, Fabian. Really sick." Tears trailed down her cheeks. "That's why I've been acting CEO."

He sat up straighter. "What's wrong with her?"

"She … she has cancer." Hunching over, she fell to her knees, crying uncontrollably.

"Oh, baby!" Fabian scooped her in his arms,

squeezing her until she couldn't breathe. His words fell on her ears one after the other. "I'm so sorry. What can I do? I'm here for you."

It was too much. She jumped up, breaking the embrace his arms formed around her body. "You can't be here for me, Fabian. It's too hard." Grabbing her robe, she slipped it on haphazardly. "I want you so much, but I can't have you."

He stood, yanking up his pants. "You *can* have me."

"Don't you get it?" She balled her fists. "I have to marry Stephan." She gasped at her own statement. Shocked really. And he was more shocked.

Fabian looked as if an expert archer had shot an arrow straight through his heart. Part stunned, part surprised, part pained. Ages slipped between them before he could respond. "Why?"

She wiped her tears and straightened until she stood tall, like a proud soldier. "My mom's only wish is that Stephan become CEO ... as her son-in-law." His eyes grew wide at the confession. "How can I deny my mom what she wants most?"

"What about what you want most?"

She turned away from his piercing stare. "Please leave now. And don't come back." He'd followed her to the door. She stood, watching him process the information. Hating herself more and more each second. "You don't have to come in the office anymore. I'll have HR terminate your employment in the morning."

Before he walked through the opened door, he asked, "Do you know what love feels like?"

How could she answer that question? "I…"

"I didn't either. Until you." His gaze dragged down her face before he turned and walked away.

Chapter Twenty-Four

I know what love is. Fabian's particular brand of love hurt like a bitch.

He didn't go into the office on Wednesday. Why go in just to get terminated again? To his face by Toni, no less. No, she wouldn't do it again. She would appoint the human resources manager to do it. Toni didn't want to see him again. Of that, he was sure. But she was lying to herself, and she knew it, which made everything all the more frustrating. Still, he didn't run to his yacht. Didn't go out on the Gulf to distance himself from what he was feeling. In his condo, he felt every goddamn emotion. Writhed in them. Stewed in them until he decided his next move. None of which included giving Toni up that easily.

On Thursday just after lunch, Fabian sat in his Bentley forming his plan. The executives were to meet in thirty minutes and he wanted to be there. He turned on the engine just before his cell phone rang throughout the audio system. Konrad's face appeared on the navigation screen.

"Kon, what's the deal?" He turned out of the mixed residential property onto the main street.

"I've got some bad news for you, mate," Konrad said, sounding exasperated. He wasn't one to suggest drama where there was none. Fabian knew it was serious.

Fabian's stomach dropped. "What?"

Silence throbbed in the air before Konrad's voice emanated through the speakers. "I was just at the gym and I ran into Bradley." Another beat of silence made Fabian antsy. Konrad continued, "He was waving around this Cartier ring. It was grand, really. Might have been the sum of what's left in his trust fund—"

"I don't need a novella."

"All right, then. He's going to surprise Antonia with a proposal during some big executive meeting at work today."

Fabian squeezed his fingers around the steering wheel tight enough to ache. But that ache wasn't near the hurt shooting through his chest. "Damn."

"Sorry to bring you bad news, mate."

"Thanks for telling me. I have to go." Without waiting for his friend to say goodbye, Fabian ended the call, cursing the whole time.

Once he was in the office, he rushed passed reception, where Davina greeted him with a smile. Ignoring her, he continued full speed to the conference room where the meeting was scheduled. With a quick glance at his watch, he noted the meeting started fifteen minutes ago. He pushed open the door. He heard the gasps, but all the bodies were blurred, except for Toni who sat low in a chair. Her mouth opened. "This proposal is Toni's idea, not his." And all the bodies became clear, sharp even. Especially Stephan's who had been standing next to the projector screen.

"Fabian…" There was relief in Toni's wide eyes and then disdain. He focused on the relief part. Sitting forward, she glanced nervously at the executives. Based on their expressions, they weren't sure how to react. "What are you doing here?"

"You can't marry Stephan." *Way to stay calm, man.* Apparently, calm wasn't in his dictionary this morning. Every party of his body sizzled with un-calm.

The crowd inhaled.

She dropped her pen on top of the papers spread over the table and stood. "What?"

"What the hell are you doing here, Pallis?" Stephan threw down the laser pointer, advancing toward him.

Fabian braced himself.

"I'm telling the execs you're a liar. This updated proposal wasn't your idea." He turned to the execs, who seemed to blend in. "He's a fraud."

"Okay, we need to call security." Stephan pointed to Toni. "Call the front desk, Antonia. Now."

"Stephan…"

Fabian drew on every bit of energy left inside him to remain still. The urge to charge Stephan was too strong—he could hurt the man if he moved an inch. He didn't want to do that. Not in front of the executives. Or Toni. Especially not Toni.

"Call now, damn it. Don't question me," Stephan barked. He advanced toward Fabian, sizing him up. Actually, outside of the professional environment, Fabian would assume Stephan was challenging him to a duel. "Aren't you supposed to be fired? Didn't you fire him, Antonia? I saw the email you sent."

Her eyes widened, catching Fabian's before averting to Stephan's again. "How did you see that?"

The executives stood then, gathering their papers. One by one they left the room, their expressions ranging from disbelief to scorn. Fabian was only worried about one person, though. Toni. She stood there, her eyes blazing. But he didn't know if she was furious at him for bursting in the meeting or Stephan for treating her like his personal assistant.

Stephan tilted his head. "I'm going to be CEO, my love. I see everything."

Toni turned to Fabian, who was gearing himself for action if Stephan continued to speak to Toni in the crass way he had been. "Fabian, you aren't employed here anymore. I notified HR of your termination yesterday." Her eyes flickered. "And how dare you barge into this meeting! I can't believe you did this."

"He shouldn't take the credit, Toni. This was your idea and I wanted them to know it. I emailed your mother—"

"You what?" Her temper was directed at him then.

"I did. I had to tell her the truth." She was so small standing in front of him, trembling with her emotions. He teetered too. "NeuRx is all you. And this CEO thing could be you, too. I wanted her to know that."

"It's not your job to do that, Fabian. You're not my keeper."

"I know!" Fabian ran his fingers through his hair. "Your mother didn't respond anyway. She probably didn't even see it."

"But I did, Mr. Pallis."

The thick, raspy voice broke the tension between him and Toni. He turned toward the back of the room, catching Helene Robuchon's icy gaze as she sat in a wheelchair in the corner.

"Helene…"

"That's Mrs. Robuchon, soon to be my mother-in-law. Have some respect." Stephan stepped closer. Clearly, he didn't like Toni so close to Fabian.

Fabian ignored him. "I didn't see you there."

"Why are you here, Mr. Pallis? Outside of completely ruining an executive meeting and embarrassing yourself and subsequently your father."

"I'm here for Toni." Fabian reached for her, taking her hand for only a second before it was snatched from him.

Dark eyes met Fabian's. "Get your hands off my fiancée!" Stephan grabbed Toni like a rag doll, pulling her into him.

"I am not your fiancée." Toni's sharp voice cut

through the air, surprising all of them.

"She deserves better than you," Fabian said with a clenched jaw and a tone he didn't fully recognize himself.

Stephan tossed his head back, a laugh billowing out of him. He'd contained himself enough to pose a question with more humor than Fabian cared for. "And why would you think someone like Antonia would ever want someone like you?"

Fabian shifted his gaze to Toni's, meeting hers like a magnet. Her lips parted, and the crease between her eyebrows spoke of the turmoil inside. But it wasn't Fabian who answered, it was Toni. She broke free of Stephan's grasp, slipping a hand through her loose sleek hair. Her jaw set firm and eyes narrowed like she always looked at Fabian before she could admit she wanted him.

"Because I do want him." Her proclamation vibrated in the space. "I will never marry you, Stephan. Never."

"What?" Stephan gasped. He glanced to Fabian who was still ready to pounce if he made one wrong move.

"Yes." She nodded, crossing her arms over her chest. "You heard me."

Stephan shook his head, stealing another hardened glance at Fabian, which was quickly replaced by disbelief. "You can't be Pallis's whore anymore. You're going to be my wife. This has to end now."

He couldn't stop himself. Resentment burned through him, activating his muscles. He lunged at Stephan, taking a fistful of his lapels. Toni's yelp couldn't stop him. "Don't ever call her that again."

Stephan shoved Fabian, making him stumble back. Bad move. It only served to fuel Fabian's near-brimming anger. He lunged again and tossed Stephan on the conference table, sending papers flying about.

Stephan growled, "To think she's been slumming it with the likes of you! God knows how many sluts you've banged before her. Like father, like son!"

Fabian couldn't stop himself from slamming his fist into Stephan's face. Blood coursed loud between his ears. He could barely hear Toni scream "Stop!" over the sound. But he couldn't stop. He felt like he was underwater, moving in slow motion and disconnected from earth. When Stephan rose, he took a swing at Fabian, catching his chin. The sharp sounds of the office came back to him.

"Ah, hell!" Fabian, stumbled away, but he recovered fast enough to see Stephan shove Toni to the floor.

"You can't stop it, you little slut. I'm going to be CEO." He stood over Toni.

Fabian advanced again, pushing Stephan onto the conference table a second time.

"Do you three have no respect for my property?" Helene's voice boomed over the commotion with some god-sent energy that would seem impossible coming from her. "And you…" She pointed at Stephan. "You will never be CEO of my company. In fact, if you ever touch my daughter or speak to her in that manner again, I promise it will be the last time you walk free."

* * * *

"Mom." Toni struggled to get up. Her mother glanced at her, though emotionless as she always was, her blue eyes were darker.

She didn't acknowledge her. Still focused on Stephan, she motioned Ms. Keller to roll her closer. "Mr. Bradley, you are no longer needed at Robuchon Investments. You can leave peacefully if you choose, which I recommend. After what has transpired here today, my family is no longer in alignment with yours."

"Mrs. Robuchon—" Fabian began to speak and Toni's heart swelled.

"I haven't given you permission to address me, Mr. Pallis. Step aside." Eyes still on Stephan, she spoke, "Mr. Bradley, is there any confusion?"

Toni glanced to Stephan, taking in his defeated stance. The pained expression said it all. "I am the only suitable CEO for Robuchon Investments, Helene. Your execs were grooming me."

"What?" Toni stood, despite her legs threatening to buckle beneath her. "You were grooming him behind my back this whole time?"

She ignored Toni. "Do I need to call security?"

"No." Stephan wiped his face. Luckily neither man had bled much during the altercation. More sweat than anything else. He glanced at Toni and then to Fabian who stood guarding her. "This isn't finished."

"I'm quite certain it is, Mr. Bradley." Her mother's voice had weakened again, exerted to capacity. Silence buzzed through the office as Stephan strode to the door, glancing back to her before the door closed. Only the three of them were left in the room.

"How could you, Mom?" A lump formed in Toni's throat to think of what her mother did. It was a betrayal. It was further evidence that her mother never thought she was capable of anything. "You lied to me. You hurt me."

"Please, Antonia. Stop the production."

"With all due respect, Mrs. Robuchon, listen to what Toni has to say." Fabian slid his arm around her waist. He held her, and it was the most comfort she'd ever felt. Tears fell down Toni's cheeks, and before she realized it, she found herself smashed up against his side, seeking refuge.

"Are you my daughter's mouthpiece?" Her voice

grew stronger as she continued. "You know I should have fired you myself for sending me that email. Don't you know you can't email me so casually? You have no respect for hierarchy."

"I do, ma'am, I just wanted you to know."

"I did know, Mr. Pallis. That is what you fail to understand. You think I'm a fool? Do you think I've only been a CEO in title but not in action the last ten years since my dear husband passed?"

"No, I don't think that."

"Stop, Mom," Toni said, finding her strength and driving it forward as she approached her mother. "You didn't listen to me about NeuRx and you didn't listen to me about Stephan. Not that it matters, you were still wrong about both of those. I love you, Mom, and I respect you in a way I don't think you know. But I would have never deliberately hurt you this way, and it's enough, plotting behind my back and lying to my face. I'm here. Acting CEO or not. I'm capable of making my own decisions and you have to trust me. For whatever time you have left, Mom. Can't you trust me?"

Her mother didn't respond for what seemed an eternity. Finally, she said, "Mr. Pallis, leave me with my daughter."

Fabian wrapped his arms around Toni's waist, giving her the support she needed after purging herself of what poisoned her life. She was free. Still, that freedom left her winded. She nodded to him because he wouldn't let her go if she didn't force him to. He glanced behind her to her mother who hadn't said another word.

"I'll be in the lobby." He kissed her, his lips pressing full on hers. When they parted, he whispered in her ear, "I'm not leaving here without you." He left the room.

Toni turned to face her mother full on. "I was

worried about betraying your secret, but you were betraying me."

"How did I betray you, Antonia? I was only protecting my company."

"*Our* company. Am I not a Robuchon?" Toni was furious at that point. "Mom! Damn it! It's like you don't even like me."

Her mother reached out to grip Toni's wrist, squeezing her so tight, Toni winced. "No, I don't like you, Antonia. I love you more than you can ever know. I cry myself to sleep thinking that soon I will leave you and it kills me more than this godforsaken cancer ever could."

Toni fell to her knees in front of her mother's wheelchair. A lump rendered Toni speechless as moisture filled her mother's eyes.

"Damn me," her mother continued. "There are too many things that I wish I could have done differently. With you. Many things." The tears dried up, leaving the determination Toni always knew. "You are the future. The Robuchon future is in your hands. You are all we have left. I'm sorry I didn't see you were capable before. I read Fabian's email and I saw your investment proposal. You're right, NeuRx is a good investment. That's why I showed up for this meeting. I wanted to observe. And, though I don't think it was appropriate, I am glad Fabian contacted me. But if you want to be CEO of Robuchon Investments, you have to earn it, Antonia. You have to work hard. Like your father. Like you grandfather before him. Like me."

Toni nodded, her heart swelling.

"But you're not ready now." Her mother shook her head, framing Toni's face with both hands. "I have to observe you, as do the executives. It might be two years. Or it might be five years until you're ready. I won't be here when it happens. You know that."

"Mom…" Toni's voice cracked.

"No," her mother barked, her lips thinning. "Don't you cry, Antonia. CEOs can't cry. CEOs push on despite what happens. They have to. You'll have to. Can you honor this?"

"Yes," she whispered, her voice gaining strength, "I'll honor this."

Her mother didn't smile, but Toni knew she was. Maybe the cancer had taken all her strength to do so. But she caressed Toni's cheek for the longest time she ever had. "I'm sorry, my dear girl. Stephan wasn't right for you, even though the Bradleys are good for us, and we them. It's more than that, isn't it?"

"Yes," she whispered.

A smile did emerge on her mother's face this time, though small. "I knew that damned Pallis kid would cause trouble for me." She shook her head and soon averted her gaze as if she'd conjured up a buried memory.

"He's not who I expected to love, Mom. Not even close."

Her mother looked at her square in the face. "The right ones are always unexpected." She straightened in her wheelchair, pulling the blanket around her shoulders. "It only comes once like that. Sweeping and grand, like a tornado has whipped you up and spun you until you're so dizzy you can only surrender yourself to it. And to you, I say this…"

"What, Mom?"

"If you love him, don't let him go."

Chapter Twenty-Five

Fabian waited in the lobby, practically wearing out the soles of his Louboutins. He paced the length of the reception desk, his gaze wandering around. The chair in which he sat that first day caught his attention. He stared at it with such intensity his eyeballs should have fallen out. After a few curses in his mind, he turned from the chair, running a hand through his hair. Again.

"What happened to you?" Davina asked once she'd made eye contact with Fabian.

"A small incident. Don't mind me, I'm waiting for Toni."

Davina's forehead creased. "So it's true then?"

His heart jerked. "What is?"

"You were terminated."

"Oh," he said. "Yeah, I was. I thought you were going to say something else."

"Like what?" Her head tilted and if Toni hadn't have come through the doors behind her, he would have heard what Davina said next.

Toni spoke next. "Fabian, please come to my office. I'd like to speak to you."

He shook his head. No way would they continue this behind closed doors. "And I'd like to speak to you. But I can tell you I love you right here. In front of everyone in this lobby. And out there." He pointed to the glass wall overlooking downtown Houston. "Can you?"

Toni's large eyes glanced to Davina, whose mouth fell open. Realization set in. Then Toni turned her gaze back to Fabian, who stood as still as he could, waiting for something to let him know what the rest of his life would look like. "Only Davina is in here right now."

"So are you." He advanced toward her. "What about out there? Past those doors. And I don't just mean to this office."

"But don't you need doors? Lots of doors?"

Fabian stopped only about two feet from her. "I don't want doors anymore. I need one door. But it needs to be unlocked. Can you unlock it?" He was in her face now, close enough to feel her warm breath when she whimpered the closer his lips came to hers.

Her eyes closed. "We aren't talking about doors, Mr. Pallis."

Husky and thick, his voice bounced through the small space between them. "No, we're not." Slow and with intent, he placed his hand over her heart, feeling the soft material of her shift dress underneath his fingertips. "But I still want you to unlock this."

Fluttering eyelids opened. Glossy eyes grabbed him. "I'm ... scared. What if you leave?"

"We all have to leave, baby. But as long as I'm breathing, it's something you'll never have to worry about." He dipped his head, kissing her full on the mouth. While only partially remembering that there was an audience, he kissed her as if there was none. He wanted everyone to know who he was with. Davina would just be the first to witness.

A scurry of people disrupted the quiet reception, except for the ringing of the phones that went unanswered.

She parted from him. "They'll see."

He grabbed her again. "I don't care." Leaning into her, he kissed her with all the desire and love he felt for her. Mouth brushing against hers, he said, "I want you to be mine. Really mine. Like, you'll need a lawyer to get out of it, mine. But we can talk about that later."

She bit her lip and laughed until their kiss fused

their mouths again. "God, I love you."

"And I fucking love you."

Clearing her throat, she pulled away from him. "I need you to go to my office immediately, Mr. Pallis. There's a form I need you to fill out."

"Right away, Miss Robuchon."

The End